Hate List 2:
Loose Cannon

Also by Reign

Hate List: Be Careful Who You Cross

Published by Dafina Books

Hate List 2:
Loose Cannon

REIGN

Kensington Publishing Corp.
http://www.kensingtonbooks.com

*This book is dedicated to my fans of the
Hate List movement who are just as
nasty and crazy as me.
Thanks for opening your minds to something
new in urban hip-hop literature.
I hope you enjoy this one too!*

T. Styles, aka Reign

authortstyles@me.com

www.thecartelpublications.com
www.facebook.com/authortstyles
www.twitter.com/authortstyles

Prologue

Yvonna looked at her nude body in the full-length mirror on the bathroom door. She examined herself, as she had many times before.

"Who am I?"

That question wasn't about the curves in her hips or how her breasts were still as perky as they were months after cosmetic surgery. The question was about her mental stability and why it always seemed that everyone she loved—for one reason or another—could never love her back.

She turned around and, through the open doorway, stared at Dave's body on the bed. A single tear fell down her face as she realized a love lost. The glossy blood from his throat dripped out of his body and fell against the wooden floor.

She loved him with the kind of love she had as a child,

when she played with a brand-new doll on Christmas Day. This was before her father had raped her, stealing any innocence or understanding she had of life. All she wanted was love. Yet, a part of her—the part she called Gabriella—loved nothing more than to cause destruction to those who crossed her path. Gabriella was how she protected her feelings.

As the steam from the running shower filled the bathroom and covered the mirror, she smoothed it off with her left hand. Another tear fell down her cheek as she readied herself for what she was about to do. Kill again. Feeling extreme contempt caused Gabriella to appear behind her wearing a one-piece tight red dress.

She placed a hand on her shoulder and whispered in her ear: "Think of it this way. Once they're gone, you'll be happy. Isn't that what you want?"

"Yes." She nodded.

"Good." Gabriella kissed her cheek. She looked just like Taraji P. Henson from the movie Baby Boy. *"Now do it. Get mad. And get even. Let's finish what you started."*

Yvonna wiped the onerous tear off her face and grabbed the knife off the edge of the white porcelain sink.

With revenge and malice overflowing, she carved into the flesh of her right shoulder the names of the people she hated most. Although the blade tore through her soft skin, she didn't flinch. The pain was pleasurable as she watched the names of the people she despised appear with oozing blood. When she was done, she wiped the red fluid off her skin with her free hand and smiled:

2

HATE LIST 2: LOOSE CANNON

Bernice
Cream
Jhane
Swoopes

Yvonna was beyond crazy.
Yvonna was beyond mad.
Hate consumed her so much that it was difficult to breathe at times. And with Gabriella being unleashed, it was impossible for her to be controlled.

Catch a Co-Conspirator by Her Toe

Yvonna and Gabriella stand quietly backstage as they watch the middle-school children act out a scene from a play the students wrote called *A Midwinter Night Scream.* Colorful costumes dress the floor, empty chairs, and equipment as they run from the stage to the back to prepare for each scene.

Like snakes waiting to attack, *they* remain still. Their eyes are fixated on two children—and nothing or nobody would stand in their way. They *have* to get them.

"Hi, I'm Mrs. Princely. Can I help you?" asks a beautiful black woman with soft, curly, shoulder-length hair. Her face is stern when she approaches Yvonna from behind.

"No, I'm just watching my niece. Isn't she beautiful?" Yvonna looks at the stage, at no child in particular.

The woman's face softens immediately. After all, Yvonna looks nothing like the average abductor. In fact, she looks stylish in her dark blue custom-made jeans and red leather jacket. Her hair is styled in her trademark short, spiky cut. Just the way she likes it.

"Oh . . . which one is yours?" The teacher smiles, looking upon the stage with Yvonna as the children sing a wretched ballad.

Yvonna doesn't have an answer for the nosy bitch and she wishes she would just leave her the fuck alone. She doesn't, though.

"Tell the bitch her name is Lil Reecy or some shit!" Gabriella yells from the sidelines. She is wearing an all-red leather jumper by Baby Phat. "Make somethin' up! Think on your feet! Haven't I taught you anything?"

"Be quiet! You makin' a scene, and shit!" Yvonna tells her.

"Are you okay?" the woman asks.

"Oh . . . uh . . . yeah."

She scrutinizes her. "Well . . . who are you talking to?"

"No one. Just had an outburst. That's it."

Yvonna has worked so hard to control Gabriella, but nothing succeeds. She is still convinced that Gabriella is real; it's just that other people can't see her.

"If you say so. Well, which one is your niece?"

Yvonna scans the crowd of brats and picks the homeliest-looking one she can find. If truth be told, not a one of them looks like she's seen any parts of a tub, soap, or water—ever.

"That one right there." She points at a girl with pink barrettes in her hair and a bright yellow sunshine costume. "She's my niece."

"Who? Tabitha?"

Yvonna can tell by the woman's expression that she could not imagine a child so afflicted being related to her in any form or fashion.

"You just had to pick 'Snot-Nosed-Nancy,' didn't you?" Gabriella laughs. "Don't be surprised if she don't believe you now."

Yvonna ignores her and says, "Yes. She's my niece. I just got back in town and wanted to surprise her. So when I found out at the last minute about the play, I ran over here. I wanted to be the first person she hugs when she steps off the stage."

"Wow! Oh . . . uh . . . I can't wait to see the look on her face!" The woman beams. "No one ever supports her in school. Not to say anything bad about your family."

"No worries," Yvonna reassures her, touching the teacher lightly on the arm. "My sister's a hot-ass mess, I know it."

The woman gasps. Yvonna ignores her reaction.

"But you should get on out of my face." Yvonna stops and clears her throat and says, "I mean, you should go back out there. The kids need you."

"They're fine. I want to be here to see Tabitha's face when she sees you."

This woman is causing Yvonna's blood to boil. *If this bitch knows what's good for her, she'll get lost before she shows up missing . . . permanently.* Because nothing or nobody would stop Yvonna from snatching Treyana's kids; and she would not mind covering her tracks *and* witnesses if they got in her way. She never thought deceiving Treyana's sons into leaving out the back door with her would be so difficult.

"Hurry up and get rid of her! They almost done!" Gabriella yells.

Gabriella is growing agitated, so Yvonna has to think quickly. Her mind wanders and she grapples with choking the fuck out of the old-ass crow or smacking her down. She decides upon smacking her, until she sees a little girl holding her hands between her legs, running toward the restroom. The glittery purple shoes she wears causes a devilish idea to enter her mind.

"Excuse me," Yvonna says to the woman. "I have to go to the restroom before my niece comes out."

"No problem! I'll be waiting right here when you get back. I can't wait to see the look on her face!"

Man, this whore is about to make me unleash! Why she gotta be all in my fuckin' business?

Yvonna makes her way past the children who are roaming around backstage. She sees a small bucket on the floor filled with costume jewelry for the performance. She takes one look behind her to see if the woman is watching—she isn't. A little girl who needs help changing a costume has taken her attention.

So Yvonna dips inside the restroom and looks under the stalls until she sees the purple shoes the little girl is wearing. When she spots them, she goes into the stall next to her and dumps the jewelry on the floor. Afterward, she uses the bucket to scoop out some water from the commode. There is shit and piss inside, but Yvonna doesn't care. She stands up on the commode and dumps the foul feces all over the little girl, who screams in terror.

Yvonna's laughter prohibits her from running as fast as she wants to while exiting the bathroom. She manages to calm herself down moments before approaching the woman.

"I think something's wrong with one of the children in the restroom. I saw another little girl playing an awful joke on her. Hurry!" Yvonna appears frantic. "Go help her! Please!"

The woman drops the clipboard she's holding and runs toward the bathroom. When she leaves, Yvonna regains her focus as she watches Treyana's kids come backstage after their roles. She's amazed at how cute they are—with their fluffy, curly hair and wide-eyed smiles—despite the costumes they are wearing that make them look like two fruity bitches. In her opinion they didn't look like Treyana or her husband.

"You boys were wonderful!" Yvonna cheers. "I'm so proud of you."

"Who are you?" one of the twins asks. "You look familiar."

Yvonna has been around them, but not often, and she is surprised they remember. One of them is slightly taller than the other, but they are otherwise identical.

"I'm your aunt Paris! You don't remember me?" Yvonna touches her heart and appears hurt.

"No," the other one responds. "I never heard of you."

"That's awful! You really haven't heard of your aunt Paris from Texas?"

The twins look at each other again and shake their heads no.

"Don't worry about that right now. We'll have plenty of time for catch up." She smiles. "But right now, I need you to come with me. Your mom wants me to take you home. We'll talk about everything on the way there."

"But Momma said never to leave with a stranger," one of them says.

"A stranger?" Yvonna folds her arms and stands on her back foot. "I doubt very seriously that a stranger would be dressed as good as I am. Now, are you coming or not? It don't make me no never mind." Yvonna lies.

Whether the boys know it or not, they are leaving that school with her—even if she has to snatch them by their undeveloped balls.

They look at each other and then at her. She knows they're examining her stylish shoes and her pretty face. She smiles. She doesn't look harmful, and she does everything she can to conceal her pleasure. Men always become her victims.

Little do you know, but the Devil has many faces, she silently says.

The taller one shrugs his shoulders, looks at the shorter one, and replies, "Okay. Let's go."

"Great! And I brought some candy for you too. I figured you'd like it."

Like all kids experience, when they come into contact with sweet poison . . . it is lust at first sight.

What Goes Around Has Come Around Faster

Treyana paces the living-room floor in their large four-bedroom home in Largo, Maryland. Her husband, Avante, stands by her side, consoling her. Her black hair is combed back and it falls gently on the middle of her back; her long legs glisten under the cute black cotton dress she purchased from Nordstrom earlier in the week.

"What do you mean? Why wouldn't you know where the fuck my boys are?" she yells on the phone at the play director from the middle school. "It's been over two hours! How do you lose two boys . . . twins at that!" She and Avante have just gotten back and their kids are not home.

Her entire body is wet from sweat and worrying. Avante opens the window, allowing the cool mid-evening air to seep inside. Dust from the window-sill finds its way onto his brown slacks and black cashmere sweater. He wipes it off with his hands. Although normally, the blue chiffon curtains dancing in the breeze would've cooled anyone down, it does nothing for a woman who is missing her children.

"Sit down, honey," he whispers, and places his hand on the small of her back.

"I'm okay!" She shoots him an evil glare and steps away from him. He backs up, but he looks sternly at her and she softens her stare.

"You betta slow your roll," he warns. "I'm not the enemy."

In her mind it is his fault. Had he not pressed her to go to a nonrefundable real estate seminar, she would've been at the play with her children.

"Ma'am, we really have looked everywhere."

"Stop saying that shit like it's acceptable! You don't just lose kids!"

"I'm not intending it to be acceptable. Alls I'm saying is that Mrs. Princely, the arts teacher, will find out what happened. We're trying to reach her. She was the last person who saw them. But we know they're here, so don't worry."

"Bitch, if you don't find my kids, I'ma come up to that school and smoke your white ass out!" She points her finger into the air. "Now you betta find my boys, or kill yourself before I do!" She slams the phone to the receiver.

"They're probably over Jones's house or somethin'. You know how they are with that video game. They probably just lost track of time."

She ignores him and focuses on her children's faces on the picture on the wall. They are her life; she can't imagine life without them. Five minutes later her home phone rings. She rushes toward it and answers.

"Hello! Did you find 'em?"

"Treyana," Yvonna says coldly, "how's the life I made for you? Is it better than the piece of shit you had before?"

Treyana drops the phone and covers her mouth. Fear surges from the top of her head to the bottom of her feet.

"What is it, baby?" Avante asks after picking up the phone. Treyana doesn't respond. "Who is this?" he yells into the handset. "Who is this?"

Silence.

Treyana, already knowing the drill, musters up enough courage to take the handset from Avante.

"Baby, what's going on?" he asks after releasing the phone to her possession.

"I—I . . . got it," she stutters. "H-hello?"

"Bitch, don't do that again. Do I make myself clear?"

"Yes."

"Great!" Yvonna says as if she'd just heard great news. "Now that we have an understanding, let me begin. I have your boys."

Treyana sobs heavily and doubles over.

"What's wrong, baby? Who the fuck is that? Talk to me!" he demands, seeing his wife's condition.

"Don't say a word to that fag. Just listen to me."

13

"O-okay." She stands up straight and leans against a wall.

"As you can see, you're touchable, and that means I can get to you everywhere you are. I'll go through hell to fuck you. Always remember that."

Heavy breaths cause Treyana's chest to rise and fall hard. "What do you want?"

"What have I always wanted? Revenge."

"But I didn't do anything to you."

"You didn't do anything *for* me either, bitch! We had an agreement and you left me high and dry."

"You need help," Treyana whimpers.

"Treyana . . . I'm beyond help."

Silence.

"Now . . . I'm going to return your kids to you on one condition."

"What?"

"I want you to help me finish what *we* started."

"How?"

"We're going to get back at all those who fucked with me. That's all you need to know for now. Anyway, I don't have all the details. I'm better when I work things out as I go along." Yvonna giggles.

"Why aren't you happy? You're married now."

"Bitch, fuck that shit! I'm not playin' with you! You talking about marriage when that life you have is courtesy of me. Cleaning that fishy pussy ain't all I showed you how to do. Your entire swagger belongs to me. And as easily as I gave you back your life, I can take it away."

14

Although she already knows the answer, she says, "And if I don't?"

"What do you think, Treyana? Look at how you feel right now. Imagine if the feeling of losing your children was permanent."

"I'll kill you if you hurt them!"

Yvonna laughs and says, "Bitch, you sound like a fool! I got nine lives, so the question you should be asking yourself is, how many sons you got? I got away with murder . . . remember? They think I'm certified. If I get the right doctor, I can kill your entire family and be out in two years. So, do you really want it with me? You think you up for it? If you are, let's get it on."

"What do I have to do?" Treyana whines.

"That's my baby!" Yvonna cheers. "Get some rest now, suga. Besides, you've been through a lot tonight. I'll call you later with the details."

"And what about my boys?"

"Listen to you sounding like a concerned mother. Don't worry—the two little drunk bastards are lying on your front porch. I dropped them off right before I called you. And check out what I put on their backs. You'll love it!"

"What did you do? Why did you give my children alcohol?"

"Girl, please! The way they tossed that vodka back, it was not their first time. I just left a little something to remind you about our arrangement. I trust you won't forget this time."

Treyana rushes to the door and sees her two boys passed out. Avante walks around her. "What the fuck is going on? What happened to my sons?" He picks up one of the twins and she picks up the other. They are groggy and reek of liquor. "Let's get them inside." He leaves her alone.

Treyana remains outside for a moment. She scans the street from her porch, looking for Yvonna. She sees her sitting in a blue Chrysler 300. A black man, with a bald head, is in the driver's seat. Yvonna winks at her and they pull off.

She lifts her son's shirt and examines his back. Afterward, she bawls uncontrollably. There on his skin is a tattoo that read*s: Don't Get On My Shyt List Again.*

Yvonna has paid a drug-addicted tattooist to ink the children. And believe it or not, he was easy to find.

Secretly, Treyana always has known that Yvonna would resurface, but she always hoped her fury would pass her by.

It hasn't.

Hollyhood

The wind moves the leaves on the large oak trees in front of Yvonna's house. Dave's silver Suburban is parked in the driveway and the banner JUST MAR-RIED is still hanging from the bumper.

Yvonna looks out the window of the black Honda Accord rental car she purchased using Dave's credit card. Her eyes droop and a wave of nausea over-comes her. *What if he was the one? What if I killed the one for me?*

Had it not been for the desire to wear her high-fashion clothes, and the cash he had stashed in the house, she wouldn't be anywhere near her house.

Before she gets out, she checks her surround-ings. Although she killed him in Jamaica—and no one knows they were there—she is still worried that the murder will catch up with her soon.

She wiped her fingerprints clean from the villa and left the torn piece of paper with the telephone number of the weed connect, in Dave's handwriting, next to his body, along with the weed. She wanted it to look like a setup; and because Americans were killed all the time there, anyway, she hoped it would be believable.

Wanting to get everything over with, Yvonna rushes up the driveway, snatches the banner down, and jogs up the stairs and into the house. Once inside, she ransacks the house, looking for money and grabbing her favorite clothes along the way. She is on her way back out when she hears his phone ring and the voice mail answers.

"Dave, it's Penny. I—I know you's not there. I—I hope things are okay with you. Please call me. I'm worried. And tell Yvonna I asked 'bout her. Bye, honey."

Yvonna is shocked that Penny cares enough to ask about her. But just like Penny has called now, she knows it won't be long before people report him as missing. Dave didn't have a lot of family, but he was active at the nonprofit organization he had started: Each One Teach One.

She grabs the fifty thousand dollars in cash Dave has under the bed. Although he made honest money, he still didn't trust putting all of it in a bank. Once a hustler, always a hustler. She is on her way out the door when someone knocks. Her heart pounds in her chest and her blood pressure rises.

"Fuck! I knew it!" she says, pacing the floor. "They found out I killed him and they gonna try and take me away. I'm not going away."

"Calm down." Gabriella appears in red shorts and a white tank top. "It might not be that serious."

Yvonna tries to lower her heart rate, but it doesn't work.

"Just get the door!" Gabriella persists.

"What if it's the cops?"

"The door, Yvonna." She points at it.

Yvonna takes a deep breath, walks to the door, and opens it. When she does, she sees a white man and a white woman outside. And there is a black stretch limousine waiting on them at the curb.

"Well, if they cops, they sure don't look like it," Gabriella says.

"What do you want?" Yvonna asks, ignoring Gabriella's remark.

"May we come in?" The man's short, spiky red hair looked messy but neat. It's a style she knows he worked on purposefully.

Yvonna also takes notice of his cinema navy Modern Amusement button-down shirt and his blue Acne Studios jeans. "What the fuck do you want?"

They look at one another and flip through their pads. "You're Yvonna Harris, right?"

She slams the door in their faces and gathers up all her things and throws them on the couch. She figures they're probably reporters trying to get

19

her story again. Almost every day that she was at Green Meadows, a reporter from one paper or another attempted to get in contact with her. She wasn't interested then, and she isn't interested now. She doesn't have time for bullshit.

Grabbing her things into her arms, she opens the door. They're still there.

"Why the fuck are y'all still here? I'm busy!"

They glance at the pile of clothes she has in her arms.

"Yvonna, this won't be long. I'm Tim Spicer and this is Mora Flasher." Mora looks like Cameron Diaz, except she has shoulder-length brown hair. "We're with Twentieth Century Fox, and we'd like to talk with you about your story."

"My story?" Yvonna is now curious. "What could a movie company want with my story?"

"Well, Ms. Harris, we've been following your case for some time now, and we are willing to offer you a substantial amount of money for the rights to your story."

Technically, all they had to do was check the court records. However, they'd been doing movies long enough to know that a script is made better when the person whose story it is participates. "We'll work overtime to be sure you're depicted exactly the way you want to be. People like you are rare. And people want to know what makes you tick," Mora says.

A sinister smirk comes across Yvonna's face. "So you want me to tell people how crazy I am?"

"No. We don't think you're crazy," Mora interjects. "We think you're unique, and we want to hear it from you. We want everybody to see what you go through. This is your chance to give your side of the story. Isn't that what you want?"

"What? What did you say?" Yvonna's eyes overlook them as she talks. "Kill them? But why? They only want my story."

Mora and Tim are filled with fear as they turn around and see no one behind them.

"But if I kill them, how will we dispose of the bodies?" She pauses. "Oh, we're going to eat them. Well, we've never done that before."

"Ms. Harris, we see you are busy. We'll leave you alone. Have a good day."

They run to the car without looking back. Yvonna grips her stomach from laughing so hard. She doesn't want the attention they brought anywhere near her. The more chaos, the harder it would be to carry her plans out. She could not have that. If they became a problem, she would have every intention of making them go away.

All in Your Mind

The doctor's office is as drab as any of the others Yvonna has seen since she'd been diagnosed as insane. As part of her release program, Yvonna has to attend regular sessions at the Psychiatric Institute of Washington, in D.C. And Jona Maxwell, her psychiatrist in the Intensive Outpatient Program, has believed from the day Yvonna's case file came across her desk that her patient is far from healed. Dr. Maxwell has cursed the officials who pronounced Yvonna sane.

Yvonna sits opposite the psychiatrist's desk on a red plastic chair. She looks sexy in the one-piece blue-pink-and-green silk chemise tie-back dress, with her pink Versace pumps. And because she isn't wearing any panties, one slow cross of the legs would reveal her Brazilian-waxed pussy.

"So how's life?" Jona asks as Yvonna thumbs

through the keys on her cell phone. Yvonna is totally uninterested in the session and Jona, for that matter.

"I wouldn't even answer that bitch if I was you," Gabriella says as she stands next to her. She is wearing a tight red catsuit, large black shades, and a pair of high-heeled, laced-up black leather boots. Yvonna looks to her left, in Gabriella's direction, with frustration. She is sick of her talking in public and has warned her against outbursts in doctors' offices. "You betta watch that attitude and that expression." Gabriella laughs, pointing at Jona. "You're going to make that bitch think you're *really* crazy."

Yvonna remembers where she is; then she softens her scowl before looking at the doctor. One check on her chart and Yvonna could be readmitted for good. There is only one stumbling block: Jona has tried to get her recommitted before. However, each time her supervisors have examined Yvonna, Dr. Maxwell has been overruled. They decide every time that Yvonna is sane.

"Are you okay?"

"Why wouldn't I be?" Yvonna asks her calmly, a light smile following. "Do I look okay to you?"

"Looks are deceiving."

"Are they?" Yvonna giggles in a condescending tone.

"Why do you say that?"

"If looks are deceiving, I wonder what they say about you."

"I'm not under psychiatric care, Yvonna. You are."

"What do you want from me? I'm here, ain't I? I've never missed an appointment. So what's the problem?"

"I want to know if you're seeing people . . . again."

"Bitch, is you seein' people?" Gabriella yells. She's so loud that, in Yvonna's mind, Jona *had* to hear her.

"Yvonna, did you hear me? Are you seeing people or not?"

"Jona, I haven't had a problem since I was released. Your facility said I was sane, so I must be sane. Now if you're done with me, I'd like to go."

Yvonna grabs her large blue Gucci bag off the floor and is preparing to leave, until Jona says, "Sit your ass down before I put something on this chart that will make any hopes of a normal life outside of this facility impossible."

Yvonna stops, struts back toward her seat opposite Jona, and opens her legs so wide that anyone would've thought she was preparing to get a Pap smear.

Dr. Maxwell's facial expression turns from anger to disgust. "Yvonna, close your legs! That's terrible."

"Jona, it's just pussy. I mean . . . I am sitting down. That is what you wanted, isn't it?"

"You shouldn't walk around like that."

Yvonna laughs. "Like what? Without panties?"

Yvonna keeps her legs open. "Jona . . . Jona . . . Jona. You must be interested in me, or something."

"You wish."

"I sure do, because if I *did* eat that little dried-up bush tree between your legs, you'd be farther up my ass than my favorite La Perla thong—when I choose to wear thongs, that is. Maybe then you'd relax."

The idea of Yvonna coming anywhere near her causes the psychiatrist to lose composure, but she must remain cool. "Well, enough," she says, trying to avoid looking at Yvonna's pussy lips. "I see you wanna play games, so let's play them. I know you're far from cured. I've been in this business for twenty years and have seen people like you go and come right back."

"I doubt very seriously that you've seen *anybody* like me."

"Oh, but I have. Just like you." She points a pencil at her. "Out there trying to deceive the world. You're a danger to society, Yvonna. A loose cannon waiting to blow. And I'm going to stop you."

"How? By lying on me?" She giggles. "Don't forget, you've tried to recommit me before. I don't know, Doctor"—she shakes her head—"maybe you're the one who's crazy."

Jona takes a deep breath and says, "I'll do what I have to, but I trust you will hang *yourself* first." She looks down at Yvonna's chart and makes notes. "I'm increasing your sessions by one more a week.

That means you're to see me three times a week, and I want you to be *early*. And Gabriella can come too," she says, looking to Yvonna's left, where she saw her look earlier.

Unconsciously, Yvonna whips her head toward Gabriella. The moment she does, she realizes she made a serious mistake. Yvonna turns around to face Jona, who is now smiling.

"Just like I thought. You're far from healed, honey. Be back tomorrow."

There is nothing Yvonna could say. She has fucked up, but she isn't going to let her doctor know it. She stands up and walks, as smoothly as Grace Kelly, toward the door. But once outside Jona's office, she exhales and rubs her head profusely, trying to rid herself of the throbbing migraine that is coming on.

Gabriella says, "I hope you know we can't let her live. She's too smart. She'll try to keep us in for good. We're too fly to be in a place like this."

Yvonna remains silent—how she wishes she could make Gabriella go away. She doesn't need her anymore, and now she is interfering with her freedom. If Gabriella hadn't spoken in the office, Jona would not have noticed her expression. Yvonna's life is on the line, not Gabriella's—who could come and go as she pleases.

As always, the game is going to have to be changed. What she doesn't know is how.

The Plan

"So what do you want me to do, Yvonna?" Treyana asks as they sit in the car outside of Bernice's house.

Yvonna's eyes stay glued on Bernice as she washes dishes in the sink of her kitchen. The yellow chiffon curtains blow around and hide Bernice's vision and the hateful glare Yvonna has on her from the car.

"I haven't seen Bernice in two years. It's gonna seem weird if I knock on her door all of a sudden," Treyana states.

"Ask her how she's doing, and ease into what I want to know—the full name of the nigga she used to fuck, the one that was cool with Bilal's father."

"That's stupid. She's gonna see right through me."

Yvonna levels a basilisk glare at her and says, "When are you going to realize this is not a fuckin' game? Who do I have to kill to prove to you that I'm serious?" Yvonna pauses. "You? Your husband? Who, Treyana?"

Treyana looks out the window for fear that Yvonna's stare alone will kill her.

"I know you're serious. I want to be smart."

"I'm the only smart one in this car. You just do what the fuck I tell you to. Let's check your mic."

"Why do I have to wear this?"

" 'Cause I don't trust your dusty ass, that's why."

Treyana adjusts the tiny microphone under the lime green shirt she's wearing. She bends her head down and says, "Can you hear me?"

"It works"—Yvonna smiles—"now go and leave the rest to me."

Treyana is about to exit the car, until Yvonna grabs her wrist. "Remember who I am. If you remember nothing else, remember my name and what I'm capable of."

Treyana exits the car, adjusts the 7 For All Mankind denim skirt she's wearing, and struts with her black Christian Louboutin pumps.

That bitch is sooo trying to be like me, Yvonna thinks.

Taking one last look at Yvonna before she reaches the steps, Treyana walks slowly to the door and knocks softly. Yvonna can see Bernice dry her hands with the blue hand towel before disappearing from the window. Seconds later, Bernice opens the door.

"Treyana? What are you doing here?" She looks Treyana over with deep suspicion.

"I was just in the neighborhood and wanted to stop by to say hello. We haven't seen each other since the case. And I wanted to make sure all's well."

" 'All's well'?" she repeats. "You sound very proper," she jokes.

"I've changed."

"I see. But what do you want? You made it clear on what position you plan to take with the . . ."

That is all Yvonna hears before the earpiece makes a loud, crunchy sound due to the mic being ripped off Treyana's shirt.

Yvonna sits up slightly, but not too much as to reveal herself. She's irritated and wonders what Treyana has planned. *What are you up to, bitch?* Her leg shakes uncontrollably as she fights hard to resist the urge to get out of the car and swell on Treyana's black ass. The only thing that stops her are the restraining orders. Her mind is running wild when she suddenly hears hysterical laughter in the backseat.

"You's about a dumb bitch," Gabriella teases.

Yvonna adjusts the rearview mirror and says, "I'm not up for your shit right now, Gabriella."

"Yes, you are. Haven't you heard . . . my shit *is* your shit? We're one and the same."

"Whatever, Gabriella."

"Wake up, Yvonna! Stop bein' naïve and you're making us look bad."

"You don't know what you're talking about."

"I know what *we're* talking about. You're talking to yourself, remember. That girl is in there telling her you're out here plotting, and your stupid ass gonna let her get away with it. Go in there and kill 'em both!"

Yvonna's face grows warm as blood rushes to the surface. She shakes her head. She closes her eyes, hoping that when she reopens them, Gabriella will be gone. She desperately wants to believe the doctors and is now angry with herself for refusing to take the medicine to help her deal with the multiple personality disorder.

"I'm still here, bitch," Gabriella says when Yvonna opens her eyes. "You can't get rid of me."

Yvonna sighs. "I'll handle Treyana, if she tries me."

"Like you handled everybody else? Don't waste your time. If you don't do what needs to be done, I'll take care of her for you. I always do."

Little does Gabriella know, but if Treyana crosses her this time, Yvonna would be more than willing to do the dirty work herself.

The Follow-Up

When Treyana comes outside fifteen minutes later, Yvonna calms herself down long enough to get the details about "Tree."

"So what's Tree's real name?" Yvonna asks the moment Treyana slides inside the car and closes the door.

"My mic fell off," Treyana offers right away.

"What is his real name?"

"Tamal Green." Treyana looks guilty. "She says he's in a minimum-security prison in New Jersey."

"Minimum security? Bilal said he had kingpin charges." Yvonna is thinking out loud.

"He did, but she thinks he snitched and will be coming home soon. She seemed scared."

Yvonna knows why she is scared, but she doesn't tell Treyana. Bernice and Tree set Bilal's father up and took his money years ago. But when Tree got locked up, Bernice promised she'd hold him down, and then she didn't. Bilal told Yvonna how his mother told him she killed his father for him. Bernice claimed that his father was going to leave her for another woman—with no money or means to care for themselves.

"How did you get the information?"

"I told her Avante is working on a case involving him. You know he works for the FBI." Treyana's eyebrows rise up to warn her that she has access to authorities.

"Oh yeah. So, did she tell you which prison?" Yvonna is unmoved by her silent threat.

"No, but now that you have his name, you can go online to find out where. She says she thinks he's in FCI Fairton."

"FCI Fairton?" A smile spreads across Yvonna's face, because this is the same prison "Swoopes" is in. In her original plan she wanted to get ahold of Tree to conspire with him to get back at Bernice, but now another idea enters her mind. Yvonna leans a little toward the passenger seat and says, "Anything else?"

Treyana backs up. Her head rests against the window and her hands raise a little to cover her face. Her chest moves up and down rapidly. She is so scared—it seems as if she's about to faint.

"N-no . . . no. That's it."

"So . . . why did you take the mic off again?"

"I . . . thought she saw it. And I didn't . . ." This is the last thing she says before Yvonna reaches between her legs, grabs a fistful of pubic hair, and snatches it.

"*Awwwwww . . . Owwwwww!*" Treyana yells, covering her private area.

Yvonna wipes her hands off, releasing a bunch of loose hairs, and says, "So you still not shaving your pussy. Even after I taught you how to clean your ass."

"Why did you do that?" Treyana cries.

"That was nicer than what I was about to do. I advise you not to fuck wit me again. You're my little dog, and if my dog gets out of line, I check her ass. Understood?"

Treyana remains silent. Besides, there is nothing left to say. Yvonna is the boss; and if Treyana wants to live, she has to remember it.

Like Muthafuckin' Minds

Yvonna walks into a crowded nail salon in Maryland looking for Ming Chi, the baddest nail designer in Maryland. Although she could use a manicure, she is interested in using her for a different service. She is much more curious about a mutual acquaintance.

"How can I help you?" the Asian receptionist asks with a fake smile on her face. It's obvious she doesn't like black people past the money in their pockets.

"I'm here to see Ming." Yvonna points, seeing her way in the back of the salon.

"Ming busy. You wait right there!" she yells.

"Excuse me?" Yvonna says, turning around to face her.

"You must wait like rest!"

Yvonna's lips purse and she places her hand on

her hip. She can't stand the bitch to begin with, and is about to give her a piece of her mind, until a lady walks behind the receptionist and whispers something into her ear. The woman looks at Yvonna as if she's Satan.

"Oh. Uh, you go back. It's fine," the woman recants after the other woman whispers into her ear and walks off.

Yvonna doesn't know that the lady has told the receptionist that Yvonna is the one who is all over the news for killing so many people.

"You bitches stupid in here," Yvonna says before walking away.

The moment Yvonna walks up to Ming, a smile spreads across Ming's face. Unlike some, Ming likes Yvonna's devilish nature. In the country for only five years, twenty-nine-year-old Ming has grown bored with natives from her hometown in China and her coworkers in the busy salon. She has traded them quickly for black culture and black men.

"Yvonna," she says, standing up to hug her. Ming's short height doesn't take away from her beauty. Her hair is styled in a coal black shoulder-length bob. She's sporting an old-school black Adidas sweat suit. "Where you been, slut?"

Yvonna pushes her arm and says, "All ova." The girl whose nails she was doing sighs, trying to win back Ming's attention.

"Just soak," Ming tells her. "I be one minute."

"But I been soakin' for five minutes! I need my

nails did," the girl continues, rolling her neck and smacking her lips together. "I got somewhere to go, shit!"

"*Oooooo, biiitch!* You get my ass and kiss!" Ming slaps her flat ass and uses broken English. "Leave now!"

The girl pushes out of her seat and yells, "But I need my nails did!" Her nails are dripping wet.

"You should think before you flap the mouth! Out!"

The girl takes a hard, long look at Yvonna, blaming her for the entire scenario. When she's gone, Ming focuses back on Yvonna, who is laughing so hard that a little piss escapes her body.

"What you laugh about? I tell you the same thing when I first met you!"

"I know, and I cursed your ass out for points in here!" They embrace again.

"I know . . . that's why I like you. Come, my friend. Tell me your problem."

"Ming, you got four customer waiting!" one of her coworkers warns when she sees her abandoning her station to walk farther back in the store.

"They can wait." She swats her away like a fly.

"What's wrong with them bitches?"

"Just jealous," she tells Yvonna.

When they walk to the back, she and Yvonna sit down in the small lounge area.

"What's up?" Ming closes the door and locks it for privacy.

"I'm looking for Cream. You seen her?"

Ming leans back in her seat and says, "Oh . . . I see. You want to kill?"

"Ming, don't be stupid. I just want to apologize for how I treated her."

"You lie. You lie real good."

"I'm serious. Have you seen her or not?"

"Yeah. She came by once last week. She move too." Ming looks up toward the ceiling. Yvonna catches a glimpse of her brown eyes and thinks she's pretty. She'd definitely fuck her, if she had to. "She gain much way also."

"Where does she live?"

"I don't know. But I find out for you, my friend."

"Good. If you do, there's something in it for you."

"What?"

"Money."

"Take a look." She flashes her diamond rings. "Ming the richest bitch in Maryland."

Yvonna laughs.

"I want something else," Ming continues.

"What, Ming?"

"I tell later. For now, let me work on your problem."

Yvonna smiles. She doesn't know what Ming has up her sleeve, but she has to admit, waiting to find out is very titillating.

Pussy Juice

The inmates in the visiting room of the Federal Correctional Institution, or FCI, prison in Fairton, New Jersey, are saints compared to the crazy muthafucka who is about to walk through the doors. After months of seducing Tree, the best friend of the man Bernice helped to kill, Yvonna is finally able to meet him. She has been writing to him via a major pen pal service.

When Yvonna walks through the door, the entire visiting room grows quiet. A blond wig covers her natural hair, and the bangs hang over her eyebrows. Wearing a pink fitted sweater and blue True Religion jeans, she struts seductively over to the man she'd been waiting to meet. In all of the pictures she sent him, the wig stayed on.

Her confidence has been high; but when she walks into his presence, she's scared.

"You okay?" he asks, sensing her fear.

"Oh . . . uh . . . yes. I—I don't know what's wrong with me."

"You sure?"

She nods, trying to win her confidence back.

He smiles and says, "Good. I'm glad you came. And your pictures don't do you justice!" Tree examines her small, sexy frame and hugs her for as long as he's allowed to, per visitation policy. "And you soft too!" He places his hand in the small of her back, and the prisoners look on in envy.

"You wouldn't believe how soft I really am." She winks as they take their seats.

"I've seen you somewhere."

"I was thinking the same thing."

Although the initial meeting is not what she had in mind, she can't deny how handsome he is for a man in his fifties. His pictures seemed so full of "prison-ness."

His typical khaki uniform and unsightly black leather-like boots fail to drown out his appeal. His six-foot frame hovers over her like a powerful oak tree. His complexion gives him a Hawaiian mystique, and he favors the actor Dwayne "The Rock" Johnson.

"I don't know about you," Yvonna says, trying not to look into his eyes, "but I like to have a drink when I meet someone for the first time. You wanna drink?"

"Take a look around." He smiles. He is desperately trying to keep his cool, because, for real, all he wants to do is stuff six inches of hard dick into her mouth and watch her swallow. "I'm in jail, baby. Ain't no bar in here."

"I know where we are, sweetie. But you don't need a bar if you dealin' with me. Where's the bathroom?"

"Over there." Curious, he points.

Yvonna gets up and sashays to the restroom. She makes a sexy spectacle of herself as she moves. A small baby vies for his incarcerated father's attention, but the inmate can't steal his eyes from her as she swings her blond hair for show.

Once inside the bathroom, she goes into a stall, pulls her panties down, and removes a large cylindrical bottle from inside her pussy. Before opening it, she puckers her lips and runs the outside of the bottle over them. She smiles.

"I know it's been a minute since you tasted pussy. The wait is over," she says aloud. She wants the scent of her pussy to remain on his lips long after she leaves him.

When she's done, she opens the squirt bottle, fills her mouth with the Cîroc vodka and Ecstasy pill concoction, and holds it in the inside of her mouth. She swallows a little to loosen up, but not enough to cloud her judgment.

Afterward, she walks back outside. Realizing all eyes are on her, including the jealous, hating-ass correctional officers, she waits three minutes before kissing Tree. When she thinks the attention is off her, she kisses him deeply. Tree's eyes widen when he smells the sweetness of her pussy mixed with the bitterness of the vodka.

"That's enough!" Dom Manchester, a CO, yells, breaking them up. He walks hurriedly over to him. "Green, open your mouth."

Tree complies, hoping the smell of the vodka doesn't seep out.

Dom looks inside his mouth. "Lift up your tongue!" Tree does, and the CO is mad his discovery ends in vain. "A'ight, but next time you try something like that, your visit is over!" The correctional officer continues walking away.

"I can't stand that fake-ass nigga!" Tree scoffs loud enough for him to hear.

"Are you gonna worry about him, or focus on me?"

Realizing he's a fool for allowing Dom to irritate him, he drops the subject.

"You wild! But I like you!" Tree compliments her. "Not many chicks woulda snuck vodka inside their pussy."

"Well, you gotta raise your standards."

"You right about that."

"Now that you've tasted my pussy . . . you owe me."

"I owe you, huh?"

"That's what I said."

"So what you need, Treyana?"

"My name ain't . . ." She stops herself from making a mistake. Yvonna almost forgot that she gave him Treyana's name, and not her own. She knew

41

one quick look at her records during the visitation approval process and she would not be able to get inside. So without Treyana's knowledge, she stole her identity to get next to Tree. It hadn't been the first time she used her name, and it wouldn't be the last.

"Yvonna, you ain't on a date, bitch!" Gabriella shouts from the sidelines. "Hurry up and get to the point."

"Shut up! I got it!" Yvonna screams, looking to her right.

"You a'ight?" Tree asks her. He looks where she was looking and sees no one there.

"Y-yeah . . . uh . . . I'm sorry." She smiles, trying to conceal the little bit of crazy that seeped out. "Tree . . . I'ma be real wit you." She leans in. "I need you to kill somebody."

Tree looks around to see if anyone has heard her. When he believes no one has, he says, "Fuck you talkin' 'bout?"

"Exactly what I said." Yvonna's tone is flat, and the alcohol gives her power. "You not in here for your sunny disposition. You in here because you a criminal. A drug dealer . . . a *murderer.*"

"Murderer?" he repeats. "What you think you know 'bout me, little girl?"

"I know you killed your best friend for pussy. Is that enough?"

"Who are you?"

"Someone who knows more about you than you do about her."

"You betta be careful," he warns.

"Why? I'm simply asking you to do what you do best, so don't act all reformed on me just yet."

"Bitch, I just met you!" He scowls at her. "And outside of sendin' me a few sexy pictures, that's all you did for me. I don't owe you shit."

"We're about to become real acquainted, Tree. That's the bottom line. You got something in here I need. And don't worry, I'll make it worth your while and keep your little murder secret. I'll give you a gift so mind-blowing, you'll want to pay me, instead."

Tree looks around once more and then back at Yvonna. He can't believe someone so beautiful could waltz inside the prison and demand such an extraordinary request. What scares him the most is not what she wants him to do, but how she asked him.

"Let's say I'm interested. . . . Who is it you want handled?"

She smiles and says, "His name is Swoopes. You know him?"

"Yeah, I know him."

"Good. He'll be getting out soon, so we have to move fast."

"Hold up," he says, with his hands outstretched, making contact with her body. "I didn't agree to do shit yet."

"Green, if I have to talk to you again about violating policy, that's it!"

Everyone looks at Tree and they all laugh to

43

themselves. Tree isn't laughing. Tree looks at Dom and secretly lusts over the moment when he will finally have a chance to crack the guard's skull.

Picking up on this, Yvonna says, "I'll even throw in his body as an added bonus."

Now she has his attention. "Why do you want this nigga gone?"

"That's my personal business, Tree. Don't worry about the why. Just focus on what's in it for you. Let's just say this, you'll receive a letter from me in a few weeks. In the letter I'll list what I want you to do to him."

"You already said what you want."

"I know, but I want his life here to be miserable *before* it's over."

"You crazy!" He laughs. He can't believe the gall of this bitch.

"Don't ever call me 'crazy' again."

He laughs and her face remains as straight as an arrow. And for the first time in his life, he's terrified of another person. A woman, at that.

"Now," she continues, "the letter will be coded, to throw people off. The sentences themselves will make sense, but put together they won't. It'll look like a poem. What you'll need to do is decode my real message by writing down the last word of each sentence. It'll tell you *exactly* what I want done."

He sits back on his hard plastic seat and focuses on her. "Why should I risk my life for you? I'm comin' home soon. All I have to do is stay outta trouble."

She moves closer to him so that he can feel the warmth from her body; then she looks into his eyes.

"You'll do it because I'll kill Bernice Santana—your reason for being here."

The sly smile is wiped from his face. Not a day goes by that he doesn't think of Bernice. After they killed her boyfriend, and his best friend, Dylan, Tree was later indicted on kingpin charges. And since he and Bernice got together sexually before he went in, she promised him that she'd stay by his side. It wasn't until later that he discovered that the only thing she cared about was the money. Because with Dylan dead, and Tree in prison, who was going to provide the lifestyle for her that she was accustomed to?

Bernice's gold-digging ass managed to think of a way when she convinced Tree to put her son, Bilal, on. Since Tree still had ties in the drug game, despite being incarcerated, he did it. The moment young Bilal started to bring in the big bucks, Bernice cut Tree off as smoothly as the tip of a circumcised dick. Her betrayal enraged him, and he had made plans to kill her himself when he came back home. And since he provided the DEA with a lead on a Colombian connect who was supplying dope to D.C. by using pregnant women's wombs, his time was cut in half.

But now, Yvonna is presenting him with a new opportunity.

"How you find out about me?"

"Again . . . it doesn't matter. Just know that you can trust me."

"I trust no one," he tells her.

"Well, you'll have to, if you want her taken care of. I know all about how she did you. And I know where she lives."

He pauses and says, "Handle him first and I'll be waitin' on the letter."

She looks at the CO and says, "Great. And don't worry—you'll be pleased with my work."

"Don't cross me," he reminds her, raising an eyebrow.

"And you betta not cross me. Those who do—well, they never live to cross another person again. And you won't be any different."

Crazy Never Dies

Lily's small body is spread out in the middle of her living-room floor. Empty bottles and trash from various carryouts surround her. The sun peeking in her window causes her to stir, before eventually bringing her to complete consciousness. Half drunk, and half asleep, she curses the rays for bringing light to what she hates most of all—the fact that she is still alive.

Lily pulls up her blue khaki pants and pulls down her white T-shirt; then she closes the shades. Once the darkness from the thick curtains embraces her, she flops down on the brown couch. It is the only furniture in her one-bedroom apartment in Southwest Washington, D.C. The ringing phone surprises her, because it has been months since she's paid any bills. She lost electricity the night before.

Grabbing the handset from the end table, she burps yesterday's liquor and says, "Who the fuck is this?"

"Uh . . . is this Detective Lily Alvarez-Martin?"

Since no one has called her "Detective" since she went on disability two years earlier, she reasoned that the caller must've been connected to her job.

"What's this about? I'm busy right now," she lies.

"It's about Yvonna. Yvonna Harris."

Lily's heartbeat speeds and she feels faint. Although thoughts of Yvonna stay with her every second of the day—even after her partner, Shonda Wright, committed suicide—she still tries to forget the day she heard her name.

"Detective Martin, are you still there?"

"How did you get my number?"

"I know your ex-husband, Mitchell Martin. He gave it to me."

Her husband left her a year ago, after she traded their vows for random sexual encounters during drunken bar escapades.

"Well, what do you want with me?" she asks, sitting up straight.

"I'm sorry to bother you. And I know you don't know me. It's just that . . . I need your help. My name's Jona Maxwell, the psychiatrist caring for Yvonna."

"Is that what you call it these days? 'Caring'?"

"Excuse me?"

"That bitch can never be cured or cared for.

48

And if you believe she can, you and the whore of a mother of yours are both fools."

Jona gasps and says, "Mrs. Martin, I'm not calling here to cause you any trouble, and I'd appreciate it if you'd leave my mother out of it and give me the respect I'm trying to give to you." Dr. Maxwell pauses and waits for an apology, which never comes. "Anyway, I agree with you. She can't be cured, and I'm worried that she might not be taking her medication. Also, she claims her husband has left her, and no one has heard from him."

"Her husband? Dave Walters?"

"Yes."

"Well, if she did kill him, that serves him right. The way he defended her in court!"

"I understand that you may be angry, but not too long ago I caught her identifying with her personality again. And I'm concerned."

"I knew it!" Lily says as she hops up from the sofa. She feels invigorated. She'd been telling people that Yvonna would strike again, and no one believed her. They all thought she was on a personal vendetta after her partner took her own life. "What are you people going to do? If you don't move now, she'll get worse."

"We can't do anything right now. I need proof."

"Well, you said you caught her 'identifying.' Can't you make the decision to have her recommitted? Aren't you her doctor?"

"It's not that easy. I've tried to press the issue

with the head doctors here, and each time she passes their tests."

Lily pours a cup of vodka, shaking the bottle a little to get a few drops of remaining liquor from the sides. She downs the remnants in the cup and opens a new bottle. Lily is uninterested, until the psychiatrist says, "I think it was a mistake to let Yvonna back out on the streets. And if we put our heads together, we can get her back where she belongs. In a straightjacket."

For the first time in a year, Lily smiles. "I like you. And because I like you, you can count on me to help."

Nasty Matters

Earlier in the week Treyana told Yvonna that she overheard Bernice on the phone scheduling a doctor's appointment for today for her seven-year-old grandchild, Bilal Jr. She couldn't wait to execute the first part of her plan.

"They're coming now," Treyana says as she stands on the opposite end of the children's hallway out of Bernice's view. She is on the phone with Yvonna, who is on the other end, also hiding from view.

"Good. Is the boy with her?"

Although Yvonna terms herself "being inconspicuous," she stands out like the last chicken on the plate at a fat farm. She is wearing a fashionable royal blue Duchess minidress by Acne, with her oversized black Chanel shades. And she is seriously depleting the nest egg she stole from Dave's house by spending so much money on fashion. As it stands now, she barely has enough money to stay in a hotel.

"Yes. He's with her. What are you going to do?" Treyana watches Bernice and Bilal Jr. sign in and sit in the chairs in the waiting area.

"Treyana, the less you know, the better. Just remember to do what I told you."

"Are you going to hurt him? He's just a child."

Treyana is worried because before arriving at the hospital, Yvonna had her running all around D.C. looking for the oldest buildings she could find. She ran into each one, feeling hopeful, but came back out, pissed the fuck off. Yvonna was specific about what she was looking for—housing made before 1976. What for, Treyana couldn't say. But it wasn't until she entered into the most run-down building she could find that Yvonna came out with a smile on her face.

"Bitch, worry about them shit queens you gave birth to, and let me worry about the rest. Now do the next step." Yvonna sees the backs of Bernice's and Bilal Jr.'s heads as she waits. "You're holding up progress."

Treyana ends the call and walks to the nurses' station a few feet behind Bernice. It is in another section on the children's unit. Bernice could only see Treyana if she turns around, but Treyana still has to be careful.

"Excuse me," Treyana says to a young black nurse who is talking on the phone.

"One minute, please."

When Treyana sees her kind smile, she's confident that she'll be able to get her because of her innocent look. When the nurse is done, she says, "How can I help you?"

Treyana put on her best girlfriend-gossip whisper and replies, "I ain't tryin' to be funny, but me and my friend was about to leave when we saw that little boy over there. Ain't he the one somebody took from some house in Hyattsville, Maryland? His face was all over the news."

"What little boy?" the nurse asks as her eyebrows rise.

"Girl, you ain't been watchin' TV?"

"I do, but I don't remember no little boy missing."

"What? Everybody heard about the lady who had her only child taken from her. Remember? The boy's father was killed in a drive-by shooting on their wedding day."

"Which one?" the nurse asks, walking from behind the counter.

"Right there." Treyana points.

The nurse looks with a sad expression at Bilal Jr. "How do you know it's him?"

"Girl, I remember a face like that anywhere. I'm surprised you don't."

The young nurse looks again; and not wanting to appear stupid, she says, "I do remember him. Oh, my goodness!"

Treyana can't believe her gullibility, but then again, she is counting on it.

"So what do we do?" the nurse asks.

"I think you should walk over there and get her to walk back with you. Tell her you need to see her. I'll have my friend walk over to the little boy to make sure it's him. If it is, we'll call the police. If not, I'll signal to you that he's not the one."

"I'm not sure. Shouldn't I call the police first?"

"Not right now!" Treyana yells, nervous about getting them involved. "Let's make sure it's him first."

"Okay. I'll do it."

"Great. Let me tell my friend."

Treyana steps back and pretends to be calling her friend, and the nurse walks over to Bernice.

At first, Bernice looks like she is going to bring her grandson with her, until the nurse suggests he remains, just in case the doctor calls his name. Because Bernice is a slick bitch, she immediately smells a rat. She wonders what the nurse could possibly want with her in another unit. Still, she struts over to the station looking more like she's thirtysomethin' in her Gucci black romper than fiftysomethin'. When she disappears, Yvonna walks up to Bilal Jr, with a can of Coke in her hand.

The moment Bilal Jr.'s eyes look at her, her heart melts. He's older and looks so much like his father that for a moment Yvonna wants to wrap her arms around him and tell him how much she misses him.

That is until Gabriella says, "Bitch, do what you came to do so we can go about our business. This little bastard is the reason you lost your baby. Remember? Had Sabrina not betrayed you, you would've never gotten into the car accident with Dave's bitch ass."

Yvonna pulls herself together and says, "Ain't your name Bilal?"

Taken by Yvonna's beauty, Bilal Jr. says, "Yeah. How you know me?"

"You go to school with my daughter. The doctor called her into the office and she had to leave, but she asked me to talk to you."

"What's her name?"

"Paradise. I named her after me."

He smiles in the only way his father could and replies, "I don't know her."

"She said you wouldn't and she's shy. She's afraid you won't like her."

His head drops and he looks back into her eyes.

"She like me?"

"Yes," Yvonna says, taking a look back at Bernice, who is still occupied.

"Look, she asked me to say hi, but I have to go inside with her now."

Yvonna looks at the nurses' station again and catches Bernice looking at them. She turns her head quickly before she sees her face. If Bernice catches her, she will call the cops immediately, because Yvonna would be violating the restraining order. Yvonna could see Bernice moving toward them.

"I have to go. We'll see each other again." She kisses him on the lips and says, "I got an extra soda for Paradise, but she's with the doctor. Want it?"

He nods and accepts the drink from her.

"I'll see you around."

"Okay." He smiles.

As she is leaving, Bernice walks over to Bilal Jr., missing Yvonna by seconds. She looks at the back of the woman's head and wonders what she was saying to her grandson.

"Was she talking to you?"

"Yeah."

"What she say?"

"Her daughter goes to school with me. She's nice," he says as he sips the soda in the can.

"That's all she said?"

"Yep."

Although Yvonna isn't there to see it, somehow she knows he'll keep her secret. In her mind she knows he'll be just like his father . . . a no-good–ass liar.

Ancient Chinese Secret

Ming parks her silver Porsche on a side street in New Jersey. She and Yvonna have just followed Dom Manchester, the correctional officer from the prison, to a grocery store. He walked into the store after leaving work, and now they are waiting for him to come out.

"You lookin' awfully sexy," Yvonna comments, encouraging Ming, and nudging her leg. "Where you get this outfit from?"

"Girl, please!" Ming says, rolling her eyes. "Bitches don't have shit on me! Including you."

"You never answer my questions. And for your information, your ass ain't got shit on me in the fashion department."

Ming laughs. "So we going to get to do my little *fantasies* tonight?" Ming had found Cream for Yvonna and wanted her payoff.

"You are so disgusting. Most people have one, but you have two," Yvonna says, secretly loving her fetishes. "I would've never guessed that about you."

"There's lot about Ming you don't know."

"I believe you. One part of your fantasy I know we can do, but you have to tell me if you like him first before we do the other part."

"I saw the back of his head and tight little ass when he walk into the store. Ming already know me can do many nice things to his body."

Yvonna is still laughing, until she sees him come out of the grocer's. "Quick, Ming, get ready. Push your titties up." Yvonna tries to adjust the outfit to expose more of her breasts and a nipple pops out.

Ming slaps her hand and says, "They good." She covers her exposure. "But he's gonna be on my ass hard. Worry 'bout that."

"Your titties, Ming!" Yvonna ignores the attention she is giving to her flat ass. "If we have a chance to rope his ass, it'll be on your titties. You don't have an ass."

"Ming got more ass than you."

"Doubt it!" Yvonna yells before Ming places on her large black Gucci shades and grabs her black-and-gold Gucci purse.

Ming struts hurriedly in Dom's direction, trying hard to appear in a rush instead of being on a mission. She is pulling it off, and Yvonna is so impressed. She would like to knight her into "black sisterhood." Although Ming doesn't have the body of a black girl, her titties are perky and bounce along with her runway walk. Yvonna is counting on him being a titty man. But if he isn't, they have plans to "go hard."

Ming places her phone against her head and talks to Yvonna about nothing in particular.

"I don't care what he wants. If he can't fuck me good, he can't fuck me at all!" She is trying to appear as though in a deep conversation.

Dom hears her sexual words and is immediately aroused, but Ming struts her five-foot-two frame past him like he doesn't exist. She's wearing a blue romper from Dolce & Gabbana, and her large shades and diamond-studded earrings add glamour to an outfit that without them would give her a whorish appeal.

She is almost to the sliding doors of the grocer's when he yells, "Can I go with you, sexy?" Ming smiles before turning around. Yvonna is still on the phone.

"Hold on, Yoy, someone talk to me."

Yvonna yells into the phone, "Get his ass, bitch!"

"You talk to me?" Ming says, walking up on him. The phone in her hand drops a little to her side.

"Yeah. I couldn't let something as fine as you walk away from me. So get rid of whoever that is on the phone."

"You very confident," she says, licking her lips. "What if me don't like that? What if you not my kind?"

Ming loves the attention and is pleased at his height and the way his body fills out his correctional officer's uniform. He's very handsome, and she can't wait to fuck him.

"We won't know unless we find out." He steps up closer and looks down on her. His mint breath seals the deal. "Now, will we?"

Ming is silent before she says, "Yoy, something came up. I have to go."

That was code word for "We got his ass. Keep up with this car and don't lose him."

"I'm right behind you," Yvonna tells her.

A Not So Perfect World

"Treyana, what is going on with you?" Avante asks as they lay in bed together. "You're hiding something from me. Talk to me."

"Avante, please. I'm just not feeling good." She turns her back to him and pulls the covers over her shoulders.

"Is it something I did?"

"No."

"Well, can we talk?" He places a concerned hand on her shoulder.

Treyana flips the switch on the lamp on the end table next to her side of the king-sized bed, lays flat on her back, and says, "Do we have to? I'm really tired."

"Yes, we have to. Now what's up, Treyana? Ever since somebody harmed the kids, you been actin' different, and I think you know something about it."

"Oh, so now you're blaming me for hurting the kids?" She looks at him.

"I said you *know* something about it. I'm sure of it. I've been knowing you for over fifteen years, and I know when something's wrong."

"Avante, I'm not trying to hear this shit right now! I'm going through a lot of stuff I gotta work out on my own."

Irritated with his nagging, she turns to her side, again preparing to cut off the lamp, until he places his hand around her throat and squeezes. Then he straddles her body and stares down at her.

"Don't fuck with me, Treyana."

"You're hurting me," she manages to say, clawing at his muscular arms. "Please stop."

This was *their* secret. A secret not even her mother, coworkers, or friends knew about. When Treyana first got with him, he beat her religiously. He took his silent frustrations out on her, never telling her why. He beat her so much that after a while she became tough and immune to his blows. Only when she got pregnant, did he let up—a little—and even married her. When the twins were born, the beatings returned. This is when she started acting out, fighting the world and everybody in it.

Before long, she stopped caring for her apartment, the kids, and her body. He grew disgusted with the monster he created; and when a pretty young lady showed interest, he left. She found solace in the street sleeping with random strangers.

Keeping his secret, even after he left her for her white neighbor, Cream, she fought hard to win him back. With Yvonna's help, she did.

From the moment they remarried, he never touched her violently. She thought it was because of love. He knew it was for fear of losing his FBI position. On many occasions he wanted to strike her for running off at the mouth, but what if she called the police and the word got out? It had been two years since he resisted the urge of hitting her, and he could not take it any longer.

"Now, you're my wife and I *demand* to know what's going on."

Only because he wants an answer does he release his hold. Treyana, nervous and afraid, rubs her throat and looks up at him. A tear falls down the side of her face and onto the pillow.

"I don't know what's going on. I would never hurt our children, Avante. Never."

"Then why have you been refusing me in the bedroom?"

"Because I have a lot on my mind. I'm not trying to disrespect you."

"I don't believe you."

"It's true."

He smacks her so hard in the face that she temporarily loses sight. "You're lying."

"Avante, if I knew something, anything, I would tell you. Please stop this," she says calmly. "You promised you wouldn't do this."

"Treyana, if I find out that you are lying to me,

I'll kill you. I'm still the same man you knew, just in a different packaging."

"I know, baby. I know."

He throws the covers off her body, pushes her legs apart, and scrutinizes her vagina. "Why you cut your pussy hair? You know I hate that shit."

"I'm sorry."

He pushes the side of her face in anger. "You always fuckin' sorry."

Remembering the words he loved to hear when he beat her back in the day, she says, "Please take me. I know I'm not worthy."

Disgusted with her for no good reason, he moves in and out of her, anyway.

Treyana hates her world lately and lies motionless in the bed. Everything has gone from bad to great and then to worse than ever before. In that moment she makes a decision: if her environment doesn't kill her, she is going to kill herself.

Nasty Bitches

The moment Ming enters Dom's house, she's impressed with his taste of design. Two huge black leather couches sit on top of Italian gray rugs. And thick black curtains, with green and burgundy chiffon layers, underline them, giving his home a cozy appeal.

"You have woman live here?" Ming asks, walking inside and throwing her purse next to the end of the couch.

"Naw, I live by myself."

He walks to the kitchen and removes a bottle of vodka and two drinking glasses from the freezer. He joins Ming on the sofa. Filling their glasses, he smiles at her beauty and her sex appeal. She looks into his eyes, removes her shoes, and wiggles her shiny black-painted toenails. "Cute feet," he says.

Ming takes the glass, swallows the liquid, and replies, "Glad you like. Now suck them."

He laughs at her comment. "Sorry, I don't lick nobody's feet. Not even my mother's."

Why he would associate licking feet with his mother perplexes her—not to mention Ming is angry that he refuses to do what she's asked. She looks at him like he's lost his mind, stands up, grabs her shoes and purse, and walks toward the door.

"Open this door," she says, holding her high heels in one hand and her purse in the other. "I don't fuck wit no niggas who can't fuck me right. Don't have time." Her hand rests on the doorknob and she unlocks it without his knowing.

"Look, we can have a good time here tonight, but I ain't about to lick no feet."

He has never sucked a female's toes, and he never planned on changing his mind. But there is something nasty about Ming that he has to have; and he knows if he doesn't comply, he'll regret this moment for the rest of his life.

"If you don't . . . I leave. I'm not playing. You never met a freakier bitch in all your-life. Chinese women are the baddest."

He walks up to her, looks down at her pretty face, and drops to his knees until he's lower than her original height. She steps back, leans against the door, lifts her tiny leg, and allows her foot to rest comfortably on his shoulder.

"Suck."

He takes her small foot and, starting with the smallest toe, places each one in his mouth. Her feet smell like apples, and suddenly it's not too bad.

"Your toes are sweet," he says in between placing three in his mouth.

"My toes sweet like my pussy. You suck that next, 'cause I'm a nasty bitch."

The moment the words come out of her mouth, with her Chinese accent and broken sentences, he grows hard. Ming leads him away from the door so that he doesn't discover it's unlocked. Once she reaches the sofa, she wiggles out of the one-piece romper she's wearing. It drops to the floor. She isn't wearing any underwear.

"I'ma fuck you *sooo* good," he promises.

"Fuck me better."

He pulls the zipper down on his pants and allows them to drop to his knees. His boxers follow and he strokes his stiff penis. Using his free hand, he pulls Ming toward him and she jumps on top of him. They are attached like a mother carrying a child on her hip. He releases himself and pulls her around the front; she is kissing him softly on the mouth. Next she suckles his bottom lip . . . until she bites it.

"*Oouuuch!*" he screams in her face.

"You soft? Me don't like soft men. Me like my men rough and tough, like me."

Fearing she'd leave before he fucks the shit out of her, he says, "Don't bite me so hard next time."

She ignores him and starts kissing him roughly again. He soon realizes that she's a handful and he might have to fuck her ass up if she doesn't calm down. Still, her kisses arouse him and he eases into her tight pussy. Her head drops and her shiny black hair sways, revealing a tattoo, which he didn't see, on her neck. The tip of a leather whip touches the bottom of her left ear and, in a snake-like motion, extends to the crack of her ass. The tattoo is beyond sexy and he fucks her harder while looking at the intricate design.

Ming handles his strokes like a trouper. The harder he fucks her, the easier she handles him. She's riding him like he's a prize horse. His thighs tighten and he's about to release inside her, when Ming wiggles off him and says, "Not yet. Not yet."

"Don't play games."

"I'm not. But don't cum so quickly. I hate one-minute man."

While he's thinking how she could've possibly known he was ready to release, she turns him around so that his back faces the door; then she drops to her knees and places his stiff penis inside her mouth. "I want to taste."

Not expecting the treat, he smiles and palms her tiny head as she takes his entire dick into her mouth without stopping for air. In his entire life . . . he'd never . . . ever . . . come across a female whose head game was as thorough as hers. He heard of Chinese women being the truth, but this was ridiculous.

"Oh my . . . oh, my fuckin' . . . oh shit!" he cries out loud.

Just when he releases his cream into her mouth, Yvonna steps behind him and shoves the heel of Ming's shoe inside his ass. Once it's all the way inside, Yvonna turns it, and Ming stands up in awe. Dom looks at Ming in horror, and a vein forms in the middle of his forehead.

At first, the agony mixed with his cumming confuses him, but it's not long before he realizes he's in extreme pain. Ming steps away from him; he falls face-first to the couch. His legs drip with his own blood.

Before he can defend himself, Yvonna jumps on his back and whispers softly into his ear, "How does it feel to be fucked with?"

He doesn't understand Yvonna's question, and Ming stands quietly on the sidelines. This is not their plan. Yvonna had told Ming that she'd come in and fuck him with her as part of her fantasy.

Ming had two fantasies she wanted to carry out. First she wanted to inflict pain on another; then she wanted to have sex with a *black* woman. She'd wanted Yvonna since she laid eyes on her; and after hearing the stories in the news, she wanted her even more. She figured someone crazy enough

to inflict pain could take pain too. Yvonna promised that she'd allow Ming to slap, punch, and hit
her, while Yvonna licked her pussy.

Now it looks like that wouldn't happen. Ming
never knew that she would be an accessory to a
murder.

"What did I do to you?" he yells, still shocked at
the turn of events. The pain is incapacitating, and
to move a little worsens the situation.

Yvonna continues to press her weight on his
back, with a knife remaining firmly in her hands.
"You didn't mind your fuckin' business. It's too
late now."

Not waiting on his response, she takes the knife
and slices his throat. When his lifeless body lays
facedown on his sofa, Yvonna stands up and looks
down at him. She doesn't care that she's just killed
a mother's only son. She thinks about how pleased
Tree will be, once he gets wind of her work.

Seeing his nut on the floor, Yvonna says, "Damn,
I was only out there for ten minutes. You good as
shit, Ming."

"Fuck that! I need you to make up to Ming. You
lied."

Ming's response causes Yvonna to like her even
more. Ming isn't concerned about the corpse at
her feet. She is concerned about *not* getting her
rocks off. Yvonna deems then that she is a girl
after her own heart.

"Ming, when it's right, I'm gonna fuck you so
good, I'm gonna have to make you my bitch."

Ming smiles and says, "Naw, you my bitch. There's only one boss in this relationship, and that's Ming!"

They laugh, cleaning up Ming's fingerprints; then they leave.

A Chance Encounter

Yvonna sits in the waiting room, talking on the phone to Treyana. She is early for her psychiatric appointment and decides to make a few phone calls. Patients who are incapable of caring for themselves sit next to their caregivers as they tend to their every need. Yvonna doesn't consider herself anything like *them*. Sure, she has come to the realization that Gabriella can't be seen by other people. But in her mind she is real; and to date, no doctor or pill could convince her otherwise.

"So what's going on? Did Bernice lose it when Bilal Jr. got sick?"

"Yeah. She was hurt pretty bad. He's her grandson, Yvonna. How would you feel if someone hurt your child?"

"Someone did. And I took care of that," she

says, referring to Dave, who caused her to get into a car accident, which resulted in a miscarriage.

"What are you talking about?"

Not wanting to let Treyana know that she's killed Dave, Yvonna says, "It doesn't matter. The bitch is getting what she deserves. So what's going on now?"

Yvonna has turned Treyana into a personal spy, and she is loving every minute of it. Two days after Yvonna had been around Bilal Jr., he suffered violent abdominal pains and was rushed to the hospital. He has been there ever since. It turns out he had a terrible reaction to the lead paint chips that Yvonna had placed into his soda. It took doctors a day to find out what was wrong with him.

"She's in the hospital with Bilal," Treyana says in a soft voice. "They're not sure if he's going to make it. He looks so bad, Yvonna. This is terrible."

While Yvonna loves the idea of Bernice suffering, for some reason, hearing that Bilal Jr. is about to die causes her stomach to churn. Suddenly she feels as if speaking to him had been a mistake, because she liked him.

"Well . . . she should've never took Sabrina's side when she had that baby behind my back. And if something happens to him, well . . . I guess he'll be with his dead mother."

"He's just a baby, Yvonna. Are you sure you wanna do this?"

The question causes an ache in her heart. *Maybe*

I am going too far, she thinks. The moment the question arises, Gabriella appears.

"If you buy into that shit, you dumber than I thought. That kid wasn't going to make it, anyway, with Bernice's ass taking care of him. Might as well send him to be with his mother."

Yvonna immediately toughens up and says, "Bitch, I know exactly what I'm doing. Bernice's fish-puss–smellin' ass shoulda stayed outta my business, and this would've never happened. I'm not going to be satisfied until everybody gets what they deserve. Alive and hurt is good, but dead will work too."

"Okay." Treyana sighs. "Well . . . I guess you should feel proud then, because he may die. I can't take any of this anymore. I have too much going on in my personal life."

Treyana hangs up the phone before Yvonna can contest. Treyana is so disgusted with what is going on that it has become difficult to control how she feels.

Gabriella says, "Look at you putting your head down."

Yvonna looks around before she speaks, to be sure no one hears her. "What difference does it make?"

"It makes a lot of difference. You actin' like you forgot about everything everybody did to you." Gabriella shakes her head. "This is why I got to take over sometimes and push off for your weak ass. Man up, Yvonna."

In the past, when Gabriella killed, it was always because Yvonna wasn't strong enough to do it. Those were the times Yvonna would black out and have no recollection of the events. But with Yvonna identifying more with Gabriella's personality, it wouldn't be long before Yvonna no longer exists. She wishes she had someone by her side to love and to lean on during the tough times. But how could she, when she killed everyone she loved, and who loved her back?

"Yvonna?" a male voice says.

Upon hearing her name, Yvonna gives the person her complete attention.

"Yes?" She looks up and sees Bradshaw Hughes.

Her heart thumps heavily in her chest. Yvonna hasn't seen him since she was released almost a year ago from Green Meadows mental institution. He'd been there for killing his wife's family, but he never discussed the reason he murdered. Yvonna was certain that it had something to do with his little girl. He talked about her all the time and felt that his absence placed her in immediate danger. When Yvonna was released, she never saw him again, but he stayed in the back of her mind.

To Yvonna's way of thinking, Bradshaw is beyond handsome. He stands about five-eleven, with broad shoulders and dark eyes. He favors Idris Elba, the actor who played Stringer Bell on *The Wire.*

"Bradshaw? Is that you?" She smiles and stands to greet him. "I can't believe it."

"How have you been?" He gives her a hug so strong and confident that when he releases her, she feels weak. "It feels like I haven't seen you in ages."

"About a year?" she says, stepping away from him. Having the ability to see from his wardrobe how financially stable a person is doing, she quickly observes Bradshaw is doing well.

Bradshaw looks fly in his expensive blue jeans and white button-down shirt by Dsquared2. It is definitely a step up from the unfavorable blue cotton uniform at the institution. His energy draws her in like a magnet; she wants to fuck him on the spot.

"What have you been up to?" she asks, unconsciously smoothing down the sides of her hair with her hand.

"Just makin' it. I have to come here for the rest of my life just to be able to see my daughter."

"You got her back?"

"No. I'll never have custody of her," he says with a sneer. Whenever he thinks about not being with his little girl, he becomes a monster. "For the rest of my life, I'll have to see her with a police escort present, or at least until she's eighteen."

"When are you going to tell me what happened?"

"Naw. I wanna leave that part of me behind."

"I understand. So how's she doing?" Yvonna asks, surprised that she is genuinely concerned. The reaction—the sensitivity—toward him is why

Gabriella hates him. Anyone who can make Yvonna emotionally available—thereby opening herself up to affection, hope, and acceptance—is a threat to Gabriella. Being replaced causes Gabriella's jealousy to rise.

"She's good. I just feel bad that we'll never be able to be a real family. The way I figure it, once I make enough money, anything's possible. Shit, if I gotta pay for a full-time police escort in my home to get her, I'll do what I gotta do. They said that might be an option."

"Yvonna, get this loser outta here!" Gabriella yells from her right. "This dude is so fuckin' whack, it's pathetic."

In that moment something unexpected happens. It is something that the psychiatrists or the medicine they made her take when she was institutionalized could not do. For the first time ever, Yvonna totally ignores Gabriella. She doesn't react physically or mentally to her words. She's tried this in the past, but she could never pull it off. Something about Bradshaw causes her to react differently, and this infuriates Gabriella.

"You think somebody who looks like him will want you? If you do, you got another thing comin'. Men like him don't want losers. Look at yourself! You don't deserve love! You're not worthy of it."

"I'm so happy your daughter is doing well," Yvonna says, keeping a straight face, although Gabriella's words are growing tough to hear. "I know how much you care about her."

"She's my life."

Yvonna remembers the last time someone loved her like that. And it was Dave.

"Enough about my little girl. I'm trying to get me a woman in my life."

"I know you got somebody."

"I don't. I'm dead serious. So when you gonna let me take you out?"

"I can't do that," Yvonna disputes. She knows Gabriella would do everything in her power to sabotage their date, only to take his life eventually.

He smiles and strokes his neatly trimmed goatee; then he says, "You funny."

"Why I got to be funny?"

"Because we've played this game before. I know what kind of man you want and I can be that."

"Have you forgotten that I'm married?"

"Naw . . . have you?"

Yvonna is silent as she tries to maintain the lie she's told everybody—that Dave, the man who would've given his life to be with her, did exactly that . . . in the end.

"Look . . . I gotta run," she says. "Uh . . . I'm glad to hear everything's working out for you."

"You sure?"

She smiles and says, "Positive. You and I are from two different worlds."

"Maybe that's what will make it work," he says. "Here, take my card. Call me." She takes the card and he walks away.

Yvonna takes her seat and tries to keep her eyes

off the shadow of his physique leaving. When he's gone, she lifts her head up and wonders if she'll ever be able to have love again. After all, it was love that sent her on a mission of vengeance. It was the need for love that unconsciously caused her to split her personalities, just to deal with life. Maybe love could reverse her pain too.

"There's no need in you worrying about him. He'll be no better than the rest. You did the right thing." Gabriella appears in the seat next to her. "It'll be me and you for life."

That's what I'm worried about.

A Quick Decision Quickly Becomes a Wrong Decision

"I don't think this will work. You don't know her condition. I've spent a lot of time with Yvonna, and she's smart. Smarter than most," Jona says as she watches Lily fuss over wires.

"If she was so smart, she wouldn't have to see you," Lily says as she is readjusting the hidden microphone under the armrest of the chair in which Yvonna will be sitting within thirty minutes. "You *so-called* professionals," she says sarcastically, "give this freak job too much credit. She's no more human than an ape running around in the wild. She just needs to be caged."

Jona frowns and wonders if she just threw her a racist comment.

"And you cops don't give her *enough* credit.

Yvonna Harris is far from an ape. But the longer she's out there, the more she's evolving. Now, I want to catch her as much as you do. But we *must* remember, she hid two personalities and killed two people before she was old enough to buy liquor."

Lily doesn't want to hear Jona's wise words. As far as she is concerned, had anyone taken her and her partner seriously, a lot of people would be alive.

"We'll see how smart she is." Lily places the microphone in the perfect position and steps back to look at it. "Have you gotten in contact with Terrell?"

"He won't answer my call."

"You should go see him."

"I don't think he wants any part of this. Think about it—you didn't either."

"Try harder. With the information he has on her, these taped recordings, and my surveillance tapes, we should be fine. Question, how are you going to get this accepted in court?" Lily asks.

"I got the hospital to sign a document agreeing to taped sessions, when I first took Yvonna's case. It's standard for my patients, and is used for situations like this."

"Doesn't the recorder have to be visible?"

"No. Not as long as she signed my document. With you doing surveillance, my case will be easier to prove."

"I got you. Just don't fuck this up. And remember, you have to get her mad. The madder she gets, the easier it will be to bring Gabriella out. She's like her bodyguard or some bullshit. She shows up, only when she needs protection physically or mentally."

"Wow . . . I have to give you credit. You know more about her than I realized," the psychiatrist compliments.

"I know *everything* about her. I was in the courtroom during her trial every day. And I still say she's not smart. She's a snake, so she's able to hide in more places."

"I hear you."

"So, are you going to let me in on what you're going to say to her? Maybe we can rehearse a little." Lily grabs the black leather book bag and packs her equipment inside it. Afterward, she zips it up and places it on her back. Her small frame and short haircut make her look like a young boy.

"I'm sorry, but I can't do that. She's still my patient, and her case is still confidential," the doctor says, waving Yvonna's file.

"Don't you think you're breaching that policy by asking for my help in the first place? And you already told me that you think she's identifying again with her alternative personality."

"I did, but I told you nothing specific," Jona says, sitting behind her desk. "It's public information that Yvonna was hospitalized for her disorder." Remembering she wants to ask Lily something private, she says, " did your partner take her life?"

"You know how." Lily's face is distorted and she immediately gets on the defensive. Trying to avoid the question, she fusses with the bag, readjusting it over and over. "Yvonna was released after all of the hard work we put into this fuckin' case! And Shonda couldn't take it anymore. She felt betrayed by a system she loved. That's what happened!" She pauses and looks at Jona with narrow eyes, feeling as if she's on trial. "I'm not going over this again! I've told the department everything I know! This is not my fault! It's theirs! A great cop took her life because of a fucked-up legal system. Now, if you don't believe me, I don't give a fuck! I did nothing wrong! Nothing!"

"Lily, are you okay?" Jona asks softly after witnessing her temper outburst.

The conversation is interrupted when there's a knock on the door. Jona walks from around her desk and answers it. When they both see it is Yvonna, their mouths drop.

Funny Day, Smarter Plan

"Yvonna, what are you doing here? Your appointment is in fifteen minutes."

Yvonna pushes past her and struts inside. Her eyes are fixed on Lily's. She hates her. In her mind it is Lily and her partner, Shonda, who caused her only sister to turn on her. When Yvonna saw Jesse on the tape discussing their family secrets, she felt betrayed.

"I'm here *and* on time. Isn't that what you told me to do?" She sits in the seat and crosses her legs. "Anyway, I come early all the time, after you requested it of me."

"Uh . . . yes. I just didn't think you would be *this* early."

Yvonna laughs and replies, "Jona, cut the bullshit. You're just embarrassed because you got caught conspiring with 'Mr. Mullet' over here."

"Yvonna, please! Don't be rude."

"It's true. Even her dead partner can see what's going on here."

"And what's that?" Jona asks. She is surprised at how quiet Lily is, even after Yvonna's harsh comments. Just minutes earlier she appeared confident; and now that it is time to fight, she is cowering and seems terrified.

"Let's see how you would put it. You're trying to *catch* me in something. You two bitches can't fight alone, so you have to jump me. But I'm from Southeast D.C. I know how to handle both of you at the same time."

"That's not true. No one is trying to jump you."

"It most certainly is, Jona." Yvonna laughs. "And since I ruined this cunt juice drinker's life, which caused her partner to tap out and burn in hell, she's deciding to help you."

"I don't know what you're talking about. Detective Martin is a patient of mine."

"She needs to be, but I'm sure she isn't."

Loving the fear in Lily's face, Yvonna decides to fuck with her. She hasn't seen her since she stood up in court years earlier, ranting and raving, saying, "Yvonna Harris must be taken off the streets! And if America's court system is worth its weight, it will take her life like she took the lives of so many innocent people."

And now, here in Yvonna's presence, she can't cope. The thunder she presented on the stand is now reduced to a faint echo.

"You know exactly what I'm talking about, Lily," Yvonna says, breathing in her face. "So . . . here I am . . . *live* and in living color. What are you going to do now? Kill me, Officer Lily? Because I'd like to see you try. I'll beat your ass faster than you can change your mind."

"I—I—I . . . didn't . . . say that," the former detective stammered.

"Sure you did, Officer."

"Yvonna, sit down!" Jona demands, hitting her desk with her balled-up fist. "You better compose yourself!"

Yvonna laughs, looks at her, and then back at Lily. "You bitches never in life came face-to-face with somebody like me, and you don't know what to do."

When she says that, a foul odor so strong fills the room that it causes Yvonna's stomach to churn.

Lily stutters, "Uh . . . J-Jona, I'll call you later. I have to go." She runs out of the room without waiting on a response.

Yvonna looks down where Lily had stood and sees a small pile of brown loose matter on the floor.

"Wow! That bitch shit on herself! Are you serious?"

Jona looks at the mound and says, "That's not funny, Yvonna."

"Why isn't it? She was scared shitless!"

"Yvonna, we're going to have to reschedule this

appointment." Jona picks up her phone. "Dawn, please send somebody upstairs immediately to clean my office. There's been a mistake."

Yvonna laughs and says, " 'A mistake'? That's what you call it, huh?"

Jona hangs up. "Yvonna, I'll call you when it's time for us to reschedule."

With a smile on her face as bright as the sun, she says, "Yes . . . *let's* reschedule." She stands up, leans on the doctor's desk, and replies, "You'll have to get a partner stronger than her if you wanna fuck wit us."

" 'Us'?" Jona repeats, surprised at her admission.

"You heard me. Be careful, Jona. Be *extremely* careful." Yvonna walks toward the door and says, "Oh . . . let me put this with the rest of the shit." With that, she drops the microphone, which was on the seat, into the feces. "You're right. I *am* smart, Jona. And I'm smarter than you too. Remember that."

She strolls out the door. Although Jona is clueless, Lily's body reaction knew what Jona did not. Lily had stood face-to-face with Yvonna before. But since her involvement in the case, she'd never . . . *ever* . . . been in the company of Gabriella until today. And the moment Yvonna walked through the door, the look in her eyes told Lily that she finally had. And as long as she lived, she hoped she wouldn't have to do it again.

Let's Get It Over With

"Treyana, don't start no shit this time. Say exactly what I told you to say. When you get into her house, place this bag in one of her cabinets. Do you understand?" Yvonna hands her a plastic sandwich bag filled with the paint chips used to poison Bilal Jr.

"Yes. I understand," she says as they sit in a rented black Honda outside Bernice's house.

Yvonna had made an anonymous call to the Department of Child Protective Services. She wants them to think Bernice is trying to kill her own blood. Yvonna did almost the same thing to Sabrina when she called the cops to report that she'd left him in the house by himself—even though Yvonna was the one who convinced Sabrina to do it.

Bilal Jr. had survived, and for some reason a

part of her was relieved. She wanted Bernice hurt more than she wanted him harmed. Her ultimate plan was to get the child removed so that Bernice would feel hurt and all alone. And when the time is right, she'd kill her.

"Don't mess up, and don't try to be slick and take off the microphone either. I'm not playing with you. Remember our plan."

Yvonna wants her to wear the microphone to monitor what Treyana says.

"Yvonna, please stop threatening me! I'm sick of this shit! You've taken me through hell and back, and right about now . . . I don't care if you fuckin' kill me or not!"

Yvonna sits back in the driver's seat and says, "Well . . . well . . . well." She looks her over like she's been gone a long time and has finally returned. "I guess you not a desperate housewife, after all. You're the hood rat I knew from D.C."

"I'm serious, Yvonna. I don't know how much more of this I'll be able to take. Sometimes I feel death is better than living like this."

"I understand what you're saying. Death would be better, but you're forgetting one main point."

"What?"

"You aren't the one I have intentions of killing if you fuck up. Oh no, sweet Treyana," she says as she wipes her cheek with the back of her hand. Yvonna squeezes Treyana's chin and positions her face so that they have an eye-to-eye showdown. "I need you alive so that you can die slowly, knowing all the while that you're the cause of your family's death. So let me ask you now, is death really better than living?"

Treyana snatches the bag from Yvonna, storms out of the car, and runs up to Bernice's door. She takes a deep breath before knocking. She knows if she seems too rattled, Bernice will be on full alert and suspect something.

Bernice opens the door. "Treyana?" she says, looking her over. "So let me guess . . . you're in the neighborhood *again* and decided just to stop by?"

"No, I heard about what happened with Bilal Jr., and I wanted to see how you were doing. And if you needed anything."

"I'm doing fine." She opens the door wider. "Come inside. I was just watering my plants."

"Where's Bilal?"

"He's still at the hospital, but he comes home later on today."

She closes the door behind herself.

She walks inside and sits down, feeling like a phony for her part in Yvonna's plan. Treyana looks at Bernice. Normally, she'd be wearing fly designer labels in an attempt to maintain her youth. Now she is looking closer to her natural age of fiftysomethin'. Yvonna has been back for only a few months and already she is causing problems in people's lives.

"Did they say what happened?"

"Treyana, they told me, but I don't understand." She sits next to her. "I keep thinking over and over how he could come in the way of lead poisoning."

"Lead poisoning? How is that possible?"

"Who knows?" she says, hunching her shoulders. "I've been out all week retracing the places he's been. I've been everywhere—the school, the store, his friend's houses—and nothing makes sense."

"What about here?"

"My house was made way after 1976, the year they started to monitor and ban lead paint." She stands up and grabs a large yellow cup to water her plants.

"Any long-term problems?"

"They say it's too early to tell. He's still young. But if it impacted him that bad, there's a possibility that it will cause memory issues. He may even have problems in school."

She places the cup down and flops down on the sofa in defeat. Treyana scoots next to her, rubbing her leg. Bernice places her face in her hands and cries.

"Things will be okay, Bernice. You're strong. I know you can handle anything that comes your way."

"I don't know, Treyana. Not this time. I've wronged so many people. I've done so much dirt.

God has taken my son, Bilal Jr.'s mother, and maybe even my grandson. I prayed all night, begging God for forgiveness. I hope He hears me. I pray He hears me."

"You're doing good by your grandson, and God isn't doing this to you. Bilal and Sabrina were dealt tough blows, but it wasn't your fault. I know they're smiling down from heaven. Trust me. They're proud of you and they love you."

"Look at you," Bernice says, raising her face up from her tear-soaked palms. "You're all grown-up. You look good."

"Not really. I'm not as together as you think."

"Well, you hide it well."

"We're women," Treyana says, looking at her. "We have to."

"You know what? I'm glad you came over." Bernice rubs her knee.

"Me too." She places her hand over Bernice's.

"I wish we could've been close."

"Don't worry, Bernice."

"I'm serious. It's just me and you, so tell me something. Why don't you want people to know that—"

Treyana cuts her off in midsentence. "Bernice, I came for *you*, not me. Please don't talk about that."

"I have to. You have my grandbabies and you don't allow me to see them. How come? Those twins mean so much to me, Treyana. And I hate that we can't all be together, especially after Bilal died. I've kept your secret for so long. Please let me be a part of their lives."

"Bernice, please stop!"

"I'm serious. That bitch Yvonna has gone on with her life, and there's no reason why you can't sneak them over here for me to see them. Bilal Jr.'s their brother, and they don't even know him. I hate that you and Bilal chose to keep such a major secret from everybody, Treyana. But if you would allow me just to see the children, my grand-babies, I promise that I will never tell your hus-band about this. I just want to be around my grandkids. I need to keep Bilal's spirit near me, and his kids are the only way I know how."

There is a silence so thick in the room that it is difficult to move without feeling weighed down by its presence.

"You really should not have said that." Treyana is sobbing. "I begged you, never to *ever* mention our secret, and you just couldn't do it. Now every-thing's going to be messed up."

"No . . . it won't. Nobody will know! I promise!"

"I wish it was that simple, Bernice," Treyana says as she stands. Tears fall out of her eyes by the pounds.

"What . . . what do you mean?"

When Bernice asks the question, a loud bang sounds off on the front door.

"Who is that?" she asks, looking at Treyana, feeling she'd have the answer. She stands up and looks at the door, which moves slightly due to the heavy banging.

"I'm sorry, Bernice. I never wanted any of this to happen. I hope you believe me."

She Knew Less Than She Thought

Bernice opens the door and covers her mouth when she sees Yvonna standing in the doorway with a gun in her hand. She looks demonic. But how can she not? She is Gabriella, the Devil herself. She walks slowly inside, closing and locking the door behind her.

Treyana passes out cold. The moment is too much for her to bear. On the table next to Treyana, Gabriella dumps the water from the large yellow cup Bernice had been using to water her plants. She dumps all of it on her. Treyana comes to, coughing and gagging loudly. The moment she moves, Gabriella kicks her in the stomach.

"You fuckin' slut! You slept with Bilal and had kids by him? Behind her back!"

"Yvonna, please!"

"All this time she thought she knew you. You ain't nothin' but a scandalous-ass bitch!"

Treyana is so scared that she doesn't recognize that Gabriella is referring to Yvonna as a separate person.

"I'm so . . . sorry, Yvonna!" She tries to sit up straight. Her entire body is drenched from the water. "Please forgive me. It happened one time. We never saw each other after that! I wasn't in love with him!"

"You a fuckin' *liarrrrrrrrrrrrrrrrrrrrrrrrrrr*!" she screams.

Bernice knows her fate—death. After all, this would make the second time she kept a secret from Yvonna about her son's infidelities. It was one thing to sleep with a bitch, but Bilal had been running around town, fucking anything with a hole.

Thinking she could exit before Gabriella takes the rest of her rage out on her, Bernice moves for the door. It is a fatal mistake.

As if she has eyes on the back of her head, she whips around, aims her nine-millimeter Ruger, equipped with a silencer, and shoots her once in the right arm.

"Awwwwww!" Bernice screams, falling against the wall. Red blood splatters everywhere.

"I'm not hardly done with you yet, bitch!" Gabriella says, shooting her in the right leg next.

"Please . . . stop! I'm sorry, Yvonna!" Bernice drops to the floor.

"You'll never be sorry enough for me, you dusty bitch. Both of you gonna pay for this shit."

Gabriella picks up the phone and calls the one man she knows she can count on when she wants something done. It is the same worthless degenerate who tattooed Treyana's sons for cash.

"Y'all fucked up this time."

"That's good, Drew. I don't think the knots can get any tighter than that."

Andrew "Drew" Whinston—a fuckup, a crackhead, and a heartless bastard—could always be counted on to do the most horrible things for enough money to feed his dope habit. He'd been stabbed, jumped, and shot multiple times for wronging people in the pursuit of his habit. He had a record thicker than a phone book. Two of the bullet wounds he suffered were by Yvonna's gun when he tried to take her money and not finish a job he started. He learned quickly that it was better to steal from his own mother and burn in hell than it was to get on Yvonna's bad side. His large build, scarred face, and curved back, which broke after he was beaten and never healed properly, earned him the nickname of "Igor."

"Well, well, well," Gabriella says. "Let me take a look at them."

She had made them strip naked earlier, upstairs, while Drew watched to be sure they stayed in line. She then went downstairs to prepare her torture scheme.

And now they are on their knees in the basement of Bernice's house. Their arms are tied behind their backs, and another rope connects their lower bodies. It is long enough around their waists to allow their backs to touch. Hot water is in the basement laundry sink and they wonder what she has planned.

"Yvonna, I have to tell you something about—" Drew stops talking after she throws her hand up at him.

"Not now," she says, thinking he wants the high she promised him for helping her. "Tell me," Gabriella says, smoking a cigarette while looking at Treyana, "how did you come to fuck Yvonna's man?" She sits in a chair, looking down on them.

Their bodies tremble as they realize that the personality they'd heard of during Yvonna's case is taking over now. And Bernice's blood from the bullet wounds spill onto the floor beneath them.

"Yvonna, please!" Treyana is crying loudly. "It was only once. You know I used to buy smoke from Bilal. We was cool. We got to smokin' and one thing led to another. My husband had just left me and I was lonely. I promise, we never tried to be together again. *Ever.*"

"Lift them up, Drew." She is frustrated with Treyana's pleading. Drew lifts them up and leads them to the deep sink.

"This is how it's gonna work. We're going to put both of your upper bodies in the sink. Now, if you *both* stay under, you'll *both* die. But . . . if you try to fight, only one of you will be able to come up for air by leaning on the back of the other, forcing the other one deeper into the water." She begins laughing, loving her plan. "But if you do, the other person will drown."

"Please!" Bernice cries, continuing to lose blood. "Don't do this! I'm gonna die."

Drew places them in the water; and surprisingly, Bernice raises her head first, and leans on Treyana's back, gasping for air. Gabriella sits back in her seat, eager to watch a good fight. But when Treyana doesn't fight back, her eyes widen. *What the fuck is this chick doin'?* Treyana remains underwater as Bernice's old ass leans on her for support. Treyana moves a little in the beginning, but soon the muscles in Treyana's legs begin to relax. It is obvious. She's given up.

"Oh no, you don't, bitch!" Gabriella says, leaping from her seat and knocking the chair to the floor. She grabs a fistful of Treyana's hair, pulls her up, and knocks Bernice into the water. She's finished with Bernice, but not with Treyana.

"Let . . . m-me die, Yvonna. I don't care," she says as water escapes her eyes, mouth, and nose.

"Not yet. Drew, cut this bitch's throat and bag her when you're done," she says, referring to Bernice.

"You got it. But . . . you got somethin' for me? I'm feelin' real bad right now." He rubs his arms.

"Boy! You's a worrisome-ass junkie," she says, reaching into her pants and throwing him a sack. It bounces off his nose and hits the floor. He scrambles to pick it up. "Slice this bitch throat first, and smoke that shit later."

Gabriella unties Treyana's hands, and Drew slices Bernice's throat. Her feet kick in swift jerking motions before stopping altogether. She is as dead as dead can be.

Gabriella returns her focus to Treyana. First she pulls her by her hair and drags her along the floor until her back is up against the wall. The smell of Drew smoking dope sickens her stomach and she wonders how the fuck he set up his lab so quickly.

"Why you tryin' to die?" she asks Treyana.

"Yvonna, please. Let me die! Because you gonna do what you want to, anyway. And ain't nothin' I can do about it," she says weakly.

Gabriella stoops down and looks into her eyes. She knows something else is up. "What the fuck is up with you?"

"Yvonna . . ." Treyana laughs weakly. "You not as smart as you think you are."

"And why is that, bitch?"

"Check my pants. Upstairs." Her laughter is now hysterical.

"For what?"

"Because your wire wasn't the only one I was wearing."

Leave Me Out of
This Shit

Jona holds the phone in her hand and it shakes uncontrollably. She has asked Yvonna every day to bring her husband along to participate in her sessions. First, she'd say work wouldn't allow him, so Jona contacted Each One Teach One, his non-profit organization, to verify her truth. She discovered she was lying. Next, Yvonna would say he left her. Believing Yvonna had something to do with his disappearance, she decides to tilt the scales to beat Yvonna at her own game.

"Ma'am, has he been missing for more than forty-eight hours?" the officer asks.

"Yes."

"Where was he last seen?"

"At his home."

"Have you gone to check on him?"

"Yes. And his car is there, but he's not."

"What's his full name?"

"Dave Walters."

What Jona is really trying to do is stir up controversy around him being missing. The only problem is, with Lily no longer answering her calls, she has to fight alone. So it is time to fight dirty.

Two Long . . . Long . . .
Weeks Later

A Penny for Your Thoughts

Penny places the hot tea on the red dinner tray next to a bologna sandwich with cheese. Time has not been kind to Penny's posture or her face. Although she exudes love to all she cares for as a nurse, and in her personal life, she has never found anyone—not one single soul—to show her love in return. Still, the selfishness of others has never stopped her from loving them all the same.

Lifting the tray off her spotless cream-colored kitchen counter, she carefully walks toward the basement, where Yvonna has stayed for the past few weeks. She loves caring for her and keeping the promise she made to her the first time she saw her—that if she needed her, she'd always be there. Just Yvonna being in the house has given Penny a purpose and a reason to get up in the morning.

Yvonna had run out of money and quickly turned

to Penny for help by crying to her that Dave had left her for another woman. Trusting her, Penny allowed her into her home.

"Yvonna, I's got your food, girly. I knows if you have it your way, you'd stay down there all day doin' nothin', but if you gonna stay wit me, old Penny gots to make sure you eats!" she says before knocking on the door.

Right before she twists the knob and enters the basement—something Yvonna has begged her not to do—Yvonna bursts out of the door, causing Penny to spill the tea over the shiny hardwood floor.

"I'm sorry," Yvonna says. She locks the door behind herself with the tiny key Penny gave her. "I didn't know you were there."

Penny sits the tray on a small wooden counter and wipes the tea from the floor with the napkins on the tray.

"Don't you go worryin' yourself about it. I came to the door afta you asked me to keep your privacy. So I got exactly what I deserved. Bumped!" Penny laughs.

"I don't know why you so nice to me."

" 'Cause I'm supposed to take care of you."

Yvonna smiles and helps her clean up the mess before sitting on the beige living-room sofa, which is covered with plastic. Penny's entire home looks like a page out of a 1975 magazine. Beads cover almost every doorway, and all of the couches and chairs, including the ones in the dining room, are covered with plastic. Beige, cream, and green are the dominating colors. Her place is warm and cozy, but lonely.

Framed pictures of her son, Baker, are everywhere on the walls. In every one of them, he looks unhappy, like life hasn't been kind to him.

"What happened to your son?" Yvonna asks, nibbling on her sandwich and looking at his pictures.

Penny, who is in the kitchen making Yvonna another cup of tea, stops in her tracks. She looks down at the floor. Hearing the question causes her more discomfort than she wants. But the unconditional love she has for Yvonna causes her to answer the question, anyway.

"He—he got tired of livin'," she says as she walks into the living room. She places a fresh cup of lemon tea on the table next to Yvonna. "And trust me when I tell you . . . I knows it was my fault." She looks at one of his pictures on the wall, takes a deep breath, and pauses. "I guess I neva could understand how a man so young could be so tired . . . wit everything." She sits on the recliner in front of Yvonna.

"What do you mean?"

"Yvonna, when you grow up, it's ya parents' responsibility to take care of you. To make sure your life is one worth livin'. At least until you can finds a way on your own."

Yvonna thinks about the abuse she endured at the hands of her father and how her mother took his side. Her heart starts to ache and she desperately tries to gain control of her pain.

"I'm sure it wasn't your fault."

"Yes, it was. I failed him."

"How?" Yvonna places her sandwich down and focuses on Penny. "You seem like you care so much about people. I can't see you being anything but wonderful to him. I only wish my mother treated me half as good as you treat me."

"Don't hand me a reward just yet," Penny says softly. "My actions today come from years of experience in heartache and pain."

Yvonna laughs. "Well . . . what happened?"

"When he was younga—much, much younga than you—he told me he wasn't happy . . . and that he was scared all the time. I—I neva understood it. I gave him as much love as I could hold in one day, includin' the love I shoulda had for myself. But—but it was neva enough. No matta what I did, he neva had the smile a child should have when they wakes up in the mornin' to witness life. *Neva.*" She shakes her head and tears escape her eyes.

"He always seemed to carry the burden of fifty mens on his shouldas. And lil by lil, he started gettin' worse in school. He wouldn't do his work. And if somebody said somethin' to him, he'd start a fight. So I'd talk to him, and he'd seem to do betta. He always tried to do what I wanted, even when he couldn't.

"So when the calls from school stopped comin',

I thought he was okay. Turns out he just isolated himself. He stayed alone so he wouldn't have to deal wit people. His grades dropped all the way down. And it started to be hard just to get him out of bed.

"Well, one day, I decided to stop bein' scared. I had to be a parent. So I sat him down and asked him what was wrong. I guess I shoulda asked before, 'cept I don't think I wanted to know the answa."

Penny suddenly gets up and starts dusting the old mahogany dining-room table. Yvonna stands up, following behind her like a lost child. Her son's story seems eerily like hers.

"Well, I came to his room early one morning. I figured if somethin' was wrong wit my baby, I had to know, to deal wit it, best I could!" She punches the table and dents it slightly. Yvonna glances at the table and sees other craters; she figures Penny has relived the story many times before. "I woke him up and he was angry at first. And then I said, 'Baby, what is wrong wit you? Why is you so angry wit life?' And when I asked him"—she smiles— "his eyes lit up and my heart softened. I knew then that all he wanted was somebody to ask what he needed. I hadn't seen him smile since he was five. I guess just me askin'—just me havin' the courage to want to know what could be holdin' his mind hostage so long—gave him a sense of relief. And then . . . he turns around to me and says, 'Ma, I hear voices. All the time. Day and night. They're telling me to kill myself. I don't know why. I'm scared because I think people are talkin' to me that ain't there. Can you help? Can you make them stop, Mama?' "

Yvonna backs out of the dining room and flops on the couch. She is shocked at Penny's admission. Penny continues, not noticing Yvonna's detachment.

"And . . . I—I . . . said, 'Stop lyin'! If you don't stop makin' up stories like those, people gonna think you serious! They gonna think you crazy and take you away from me! Do you want that?' And when I did that, when I said those hateful words to him, I took away the lil life he managed to use to just walk around this world. He was left wit nothin'."

When Penny turns around and looks at Yvonna, her eyes are bloodshot red and filled with tears. "I didn't believe my son, and I killed him. If I had believed him, he neva woulda placed the barrel of my gun to his head and killed himself."

"That bitch is fucking crazy! And you're stupid as shit if you listen to her. She's probably some lesbian tryin' to get you to fuck her old ass or somethin'. And don't think for one minute I'm going to stay around and watch that nasty shit either." Gabriella appears on Yvonna's right.

"Shut up!" Yvonna yells.

"You shut up and look at yourself. If you believe that old slut, I'll hurt her. Don't make me do it, Yvonna. You know I'm not playin'!"

"You leave her alone! If you hurt her, I'll kill

you!" Yvonna yells, fearful of what her mental condition might make her do.

Looking at Penny, Yvonna says, "Penny, I have to talk to you. I . . . don't think it's a good idea for me to stay here. I don't want to hurt you." Yvonna surprises herself by caring for Penny, and for defying Gabriella.

"She can't hurt me," Penny says softly. "She can't hurt me because she's you, and I know you want to get better. And you don't have to go through none of dis alone. I've studied your case. Them white folks gots medicine for stuff like this. But you gots to take it." Penny disappears into the kitchen, opens the top of a blue cookie jar, and removes a pill bottle. She walks back to the couch. "I gots this from the hospital, the day you called me and told me you needed a place to stay. I'm not s'posed to have it, and I'll answa to God for my sins for stealin'. But I know if you take it, you'll be betta. And you'll be able to live your life. Ain't that what you want?"

Penny looks into Yvonna's eyes and sees sorrow. The energy Yvonna shows matches her son's exactly when he asked for help and she denied him.

And suddenly, as if Penny had said the most hateful thing imaginable to Yvonna, her face changes.

"Bitch, you don't know who you're fuckin' wit!"

Unmoved by the presence of Yvonna's multiple personality disorder, Penny straightens her spine and lifts her head.

"Yvonna, you're still wit me, baby." She grabs

her hand forcefully to take control of the situation. "This is you. You're one person. Not two. And you're still wit me right now."

Gabriella snatches her hand away and says, "Bitch, you betta stay out of my life! I'm warnin' you."

With that, she gets up and storms out of the house. Little does she know, but staying out of her life is the last thing Penny is planning to do.

Somebody Else
Outside of Herself

Yvonna's mind rushes. She always felt close to Penny; but after hearing her son's story, she feels even closer to her. She realizes she must talk to Penny to warn her that caring for her might place her life in danger. It is as if her soul is divided in half. One part loves Penny, and the other part hates her for making her trust anyone outside of herself.

Yvonna hops out of a cab in front of the Duke Ellington Campus. The sun shines brightly. "Stay right here, I won't be long," she tells the cabdriver.

Slowly she moves past the other students, keeping her distance from her intended target, her fourteen-year-old sister, Jesse. Although Jhane moves Jesse from place to place to keep Yvonna away from her, it doesn't work. Jesse is the one person nobody can keep her away from.

Yvonna walks closer to Jesse's locker and smiles. She's been there many times before and knows Jesse's routine perfectly. Although Jesse has lost a limb, she's happy when she sees her new prosthetic arm. Yvonna found out a year earlier that Johns Hopkins had developed a procedure to create a prosthesis that could listen to the brain to provide patients with more fluid motions. She sent the clip to Jhane anonymously so that Jesse could know about the procedure. It pleases her that the masculine bitch took her advice.

Jesse is surrounded by a bunch of girls, and it's apparent that she is popular in school. Her confidence has grown, and she is now so beautiful that it is hard not to spot her in a crowded room. When the bell rings, Jesse and her friends focus on their lockers, grabbing what they need for class. The other kids scatter everywhere to make their classes on time.

But Jesse isn't speeding. She stops and looks directly at Yvonna. Jesse's eyes widen; but this time she doesn't run. Instead, she walks up to Yvonna.

"You haven't been here in a few days. I thought you finally left me alone," she says softly. "I guess I was wrong."

"You know I've been watching you?"

"Yvonna, it's hard not to see you. Look how you're dressed," she points out.

Yvonna takes notice of the black silk Roberto Cavalli dress, with the embedded silk scarf belt she is wearing.

"I guess the dress is a bit much, huh?"

"The Cavalli? I'm talking about the red sequin Nina Ricci shoes!" Jesse laughs.

At that moment Yvonna's heart skips. She is actually having a conversation with her baby sister, and Jesse isn't running.

"Wait a minute. What do you know about fashion?"

"After running from you all my life, I had to learn something about you," she says with disappointment. Her head drops and she readjusts her book bag, saying, "Look . . . please don't follow me. I like it here, Yvonna. I have friends and I'm really good at singing. My life has changed."

"You sing? I didn't know."

"I'm working on an album, and everything."

"That's great! I'm happy for you."

"Thank you. But are you *really* happy for me?"

"Yes, Jesse, I am."

"Good. So please don't come back. If Jhane finds out you've been following me again, she'll move me. I'll lose everything."

Yvonna's face becomes angry.

"Please don't hurt her, Yvonna. I love her. She's taken care of me and I feel happy with her. Okay?"

All Yvonna wants to do is murder the beastly woman known as "Aunt Jhane." In fact, she has plans to see her later that week.

"I'm not like that anymore, Jesse. I just came to see you."

"Good." Jesse smiles. She turns around to walk

away, but she stops and looks at her sister. "How are you?"

Yvonna's stomach flutters and one tear forms in the wells of her eyes. Her sister actually cares enough to ask how she is.

"Uh . . . I'm fine. Thanks for asking."

"Great." Jesse smiles. "I'm happy to hear you're doing good."

Without another word Jesse walks away, leaving Yvonna alone. Yvonna is tempted to run behind her, to convince her to play hooky from school. There is so much that she wants to know. Like, does she have a boyfriend? Is she in any trouble she could help her with? And does she miss her a little?

Just speaking to Jesse causes her to think about being a better person. But when she walks out of the building, and toward her cab, hate consumes Yvonna all over again. Because outside the school sits five police cars. And they all have one goal: to take one crazy-ass bitch into police custody.

Not This Shit Again

The interrogation room in Washington, D.C., is hot, but Yvonna remains cool. She learned a long time ago that if you're under investigation, your interview starts the moment you walk through the door.

The two officers, on the other hand, are losing their cool. It has been over an hour, and Yvonna has stuck to her guns. They have tried to break her down using old methods, and all have failed. Someone should have told them that Yvonna Harris is not the normal suspect.

"So let me get this straight. You expect us to believe that you don't know where your husband is? You expect us to believe he just fell off of the face of the earth?" Officer Jensen asks.

Peter Jensen's white complexion flushes red and his large nose is dripping with sweat, giving him a glossy glow. Although he isn't all that attractive, compared to his partner, Guy Samuels, he looks like a male model. If nothing else, Peter's body is in supreme shape.

"Peter, if you're going to ask me a question over and over again, at least change it up a little," Yvonna says, crossing her legs. " 'Cause to tell you the truth, I'm getting bored with it all."

"I don't care if you're getting bored or not! I want answers."

"And I gave you one. I'm sorry if it's not to your liking. I have not seen him since he left me."

"You expect us to believe that?" Officer Samuels says, sitting on a seat directly on the left of her. He is overweight and breathing heavily. His dark skin is ashy and he looks dusty. It doesn't help that his thick mustache makes it difficult to understand what he is saying.

"I know you look at me and say to yourself, 'If I ever got a chance to sleep with her dirty panties under my nose, I'd rather cut my dick off than leave.' But what you have to realize is this. . . . A man like you didn't leave me because a man like you never had a chance with me. Dave was different," she states, smirking.

" 'Was'? You sound like he's gone forever," Samuels says.

"Yes. He *was* with me. Now he's *not*."

"You think you're smart, don't you?"

"Officer . . . what do you want? You're wastin' my time."

Officer Samuels opens another folder and says, "What do you know about the disappearances of Bernice Santana and Treyana Plier?"

"I'm not interested in either one of them. I thought you were questioning me on my husband, so why are you still bringing that up? I don't know anything about them."

"So you want us to believe you haven't been in Treyana's presence?" Jensen asks.

"I didn't say that. I said I'm not interested in either one of them. And I don't know anything about their disappearances, and it's obvious you don't either. Now look . . . if you fellas are not going to charge me, I have a beer to drink and a dick to fuck. I would like to go about my business."

"With your husband?"

"I just said we're not together, mister."

"No, you didn't. You said you hadn't heard from him." Jensen continues thinking that he's onto something.

Yvonna laughs, shakes her head, and says, "You do the worst job of trying to entrap somebody I've ever seen in my life. Let me give you a few pointers. Before you can begin to entrap someone, you must ask the right questions, at the right times."

"Lady, I don't know what you're talking about. I'm not trying to entrap you. I'm simply doing my job. And that is, trying to find the whereabouts of three missing people. And you're sitting here, lying, saying that you didn't hear from them."

Yvonna leans in toward him, licks her lips, and says, "Now, when did I say I didn't hear from them?"

"You said it when we—"

"When we *what*? Do you even know what you're saying?" Yvonna interrupts him.

"Yes, you said it earlier when we . . . No . . . you just said it right before I asked you the initial question."

"So I said it when you asked me the initial question? What was your initial question?"

"I asked you . . . uh . . . did you hear from Plier? And you said you hadn't heard from her."

"Are you sure I said I didn't hear from her . . . or did I say I'm not interested in her? Which one is it, Officer?"

"It was when . . . Wait . . . I asked you after you said—"

"After I said what, Officer?" Yvonna interrupts once more. She leans back on her seat and smiles at how unraveled he has become.

"Look . . . I said I hadn't talked or asked you the initial question before you came in."

"Do you even know what you're sayin'?"

"I know what I'm saying. You're just trying to mess me—"

"I'm trying to mess you what," she interjects.

"I know what you're doing, young lady. And although my partner might be tripping over his own feet a little, I know *exactly* what I want to know. And what I want to know is this. . . . Where the fuck is Dave Walters, Bernice Santana, and Trey-ana Plier?"

Yvonna smiles at how Samuels stops her from making his partner look like an idiot.

"Like I said, I won't be able to help you because I'm not interested in any one of them. And as a contingency of my release, I'm not even allowed to be around Bernice Santana."

"Breaking the law has never stopped you before."

"You don't know me. So don't believe everything you read in the papers."

Officer Samuels is just about to dig deeper into his investigation when an older black man opens the door and says, "Samuels, I have to talk to you for a minute."

"Not now, man. I'm in a meeting."

"This is serious," he says, lowering his voice. "You told me to let you know right away when we got a break. We have one."

Officer Samuels pushes his chair back, stands up, and says, "Think about what I said, young lady. This is serious. And we can't help you, if you don't help us."

Samuels meets the other man at the door. The man's face is bunched up and he obviously has something urgent to tell him, which can't wait.

"They found her." He tries his best to whisper, but Yvonna's ear-hustling skills are impeccable. She hears everything.

"What do you mean they found her?" he asks, moving in closer.

"They found her. In her house. In a makeshift storm shelter below the house."

"But we tore her house upside down! It's impossible for her to be inside!" he yells. Spit escapes his mouth and he looks like a wild animal about to attack.

"Apparently, you didn't tear it up too good. The man said they found her," Yvonna chimes in. He turns around and looks at Yvonna, who wears a smirk on her face.

"I wouldn't laugh just yet," he says before focusing back on the officer. "Was anybody with her?"

"Yes."

"Who? Plier?"

"No. It was a man."

Samuels holds up the wall for support. He feels foolish that his investigators had not only missed Bernice's body, but also another victim. His head is spinning so fast that he is afraid to ask another question, for fear that he'll get the answer. "Who is he?"

"We don't know. They're trying to get his identity. But there's more."

Jensen walks over to the commotion and listens.

"What else is it?" Samuels asks.

"Her head . . . uh . . . was . . . chopped off, and . . ." The bearer of bad news turns away from the men. He is about to vomit and wants to spare them if he can. "The male vic was on the floor, completely nude. His penis was in the victim's mouth. He looked like he suffered a drug overdose. There was a lot of blood under his nose."

The three men look at Yvonna, who is laughing so hard that she almost falls out of her seat. They know she has everything to do with it; but with the way the murder scene was set up, it places her in the clear.

"I'm glad you think it's funny," Jensen says angrily. "But don't forget, we still haven't found Plier."

"That sounds like a problem that belongs to you, not me, Officer. But unless you have a case against me, I suggest you let me go before you have a problem you won't be able to afford."

The men look at each other, knowing what they have to do. Neither of them wants to admit it, but she is right. Without evidence, there is nothing they can do. So they do the inevitable and let her go.

Here I Am Again

Yvonna is sitting upon the large leather recliner as her feet rest in the bowl that is full of warm soapy water. Ming is busy mixing a special purple nail color just for Yvonna, who doesn't want anybody in the world having shades like hers.

"Ming, hurry up and bring your Chinky-eyed ass over here! My water's getting cold!"

"Shut up! You ask me to do something and then fuss! I'm coming, you impatient heffa!"

Yvonna laughs at the way Ming curses and talks trash. Yvonna is teaching her the proper way to lay a bitch out, but Ming still isn't getting it.

"You gettin' better, bitch. Still need work, though."

Ming laughs. "Fuck you!"

Yvonna tunes her out and focuses back on her letter. She finally has finished composing it and wants to make sure it is perfect. After all, she is planning a murder and torture. With Bernice dead, she can move on to Swoopes.

You gonna wish you ain't fuck wit me! Yvonna thinks.

Ming sits in front of her and says, "Give your feet! But don't wet up my outfit."

"I'm not thinking about your outfit."

"So, Yvonna, I give to you information. What are you going to do now?"

"You don't wanna know all of that."

"I do. I'm very interested."

"I got my ideas."

"So when you give to me my fantasy?"

"Soon, Ming."

"How soon?"

"Soon! Look, I hope you don't think we to-gether or know shit like that just because of our arrangement."

"I'm not thinkin' about you. I just want you to make good on deal."

"I got you." Yvonna focuses on the letter again. "Ming, let me read something to you. Tell me what you think."

"Go ahead," she says as she carves the cuticles around Yvonna's toenails.

Yvonna clears her throat and reads the poem:

> *You are I.*
> *And you are what I want.*
> *I am her who can't live without him.*
> *You are my heart beat.*

I'd rather be raped
And
I'd rather be tortured
Until I say when.
Because it's
Not going to do me any good at all
To be without you. I said
That until it's all said and
Done
That you are what I
Want.
You . . . not him.
When you left, I felt killed.

Ming stops working on her feet and says, "That's it?"

"Yeah. What you think?"

"That's no poem! That's stupid! That means nothin'!"

Yvonna laughs. "It ain't hardly stupid. And trust me, it definitely means something."

Sure, the poem was not her best work, but she was sure that if Tree listened and followed her instructions by reading the last word of each sentence it would read: *I want him beat, raped, and tortured. When it's all said and done, I want him killed.*

After she is done with the letter, she folds it, places it in an envelope, and licks it shut. A smile comes across her face because Swoopes is one of the main people she wants to kill personally. She still remembers how he and his friends raped and beat her, only to leave her for dead in an abandoned house. So she desires nothing more than that same fate to happen to him. Had it not been for her deceased husband, Dave, she would not be alive.

When Dave enters her mind, she is overwhelmed with loneliness and horniness. Murder always does arouse her. It tugs at her even more when she sees Ming at the sink, kissing one of her jump-off dudes she fucks from time to time.

"Ming, hurry the fuck up! I got somewhere to be!" Yvonna hates looking at the fine-ass nigga Ming's face sucking.

Ming puts her middle finger up in the air.

"If I listen to that weak-ass poem, you can give to me five minutes."

"Flat-ass bitch!"

Yvonna sighs and throws her head onto the headrest. It has been so long since she has had a man's company . . . a man's companionship . . . a man's dick. And then she remembers . . . Bradshaw. She pulls out his card and decides to give him a call.

The phone rings twice before he says, "Yvonna, I was waiting on you to call."

She smiles and says, "And how did you know it was me?"

"Because I gave you a number I just got the day we met. I haven't even given it to anyone yet. When it rang for the first time, I wanted you to be the first to call."

Yvonna takes notice of his tone and conversation. He sounds a little too soft for her liking. She is used to roughnecks, and Bradshaw puts her in mind of the good doctor Terrell she lived with in Baltimore. She couldn't stand him.

"Are you at work or somethin'?" she asks, turned off by him already.

"Yeah. Why you ask?"

"It figures," she says, rolling her eyes.

"Where are you? Let me take you out."

"I'm in the nail salon in Hyattsville."

"Cool. Meet me at the bookstore in Eastover Shopping Center."

Did this nigga just say "cool" and "bookstore" in the same sentence? she thinks.

"Bookstore? That's not my idea of a first date."

He laughs and says, "I know, but trust me, they have a nice setup in there. We'll be able to drink some coffee, sit back, and relax. What do you say?"

Although she wasn't the reading or talking type, she did have to admit that his idea was original.

"I'll be there in thirty minutes. You did say Eastover, right?"

"Yeah. It's Cartel Café and Books in Oxon Hill, Maryland. I'll see you in a minute."

She hangs up the phone and looks at Ming. For some reason Yvonna is growing jealous of the attention Ming is giving her male friend. It isn't that Yvonna is into her; she just hates that Ming isn't focused on her.

"Ming! Come on!" she yells.

Both the fine-ass nigga and Ming look at her. You can tell he doesn't like that Yvonna keeps calling her, despite Ming being at work. She decides to fuck with him also.

"Wait. Two more minutes," Ming answers.

"If you come now, I'll give you what you've been asking for."

Ming looks at the guy, says one word to him, and walks away. He looks at Yvonna, shakes his head, and walks out of the nail salon.

"You not play, are you?"

"There's only one way to find out."

Yvonna laughs and sinks onto her seat, having claimed defeat when she realizes she hasn't split into Gabriella in a day. This is odd. Because whenever she expresses deep emotion or concern for anybody, her personal hater Gabriella appears. Something is definitely going on.

She looks at her watch and notices it is four-thirty. That means she'll have about two hours to spend with Bradshaw before she has to rush home and take caution to keep her little secret: Treyana, in Penny's basement. She can't risk Penny finding out that Treyana is in her home.

Gabriella has been with her ever since they left Bernice's. It made her angry to discover that Treyana had been recording Yvonna's conversations. The only upside was, when Gabriella drenched

Treyana with the water from the yellow cup, the cheap tape recorder broke immediately. It was far from the wire Treyana had bragged about. And for her consistent betrayal, Gabriella made her pay greatly.

"When are you due, pretty eyes?" the cashier says to one of her customers. The pretty, dark-skinned woman has eyes as shiny as marbles and is nine months pregnant.

"In a month, girl. But let me get out of here and read my books. I'll check you later. I'll probably be finished with these in a day."

Yvonna sighs, irritated with both of them bitches. "I wish the fuck she takes them home and read 'em then!" she says to Bradshaw, who doesn't co-sign.

When the pretty, pregnant lady leaves, the cashier rings up Brad's purchase.

"You want anything?" he asks Yvonna as he pays for his.

"No, I'm good."

He pays for his purchases and they walk to the back of the store to sit on one of the large black leather sofas.

"So, tell me, what have you been up to?"

"Nothin'," she says, hating the getting-to-know process. "Look . . . haven't we gone through all this at the clinic?"

"All what?"

"You know . . . the small-talk bullshit."

Bradshaw's eyebrows rise. "Come again."

She sighs and says, "Bradshaw, I'ma be real with you. I'm trying to fuck. Now this bookstore is cute and all, but unless these people gonna let me jump on your dick back here, I'm trying to leave. So what's up?"

He almost spills the coffee over the floor when he hears her comment. "Come again."

"I said, I'm trying to fuck."

"Uh . . . Yvonna, I wasn't trying to disrespect you. I was trying to . . ." He stops after she rolls her eyes.

"Look, I'm used to a thug-ass nigga. And if you gonna be 'Mr. Romeo,' you need one of them meek-lookin' bitches at the register. Because, trust me, I'm not gonna be able to bump wit you."

Bradshaw looks at her with confusion at first. But as if someone had changed the channel, his entire personality flips. Without saying a word, he suddenly seems as if he's been possessed with swag.

Bradshaw stands up, adjusts his pants, and says, "Fuck you sittin' down for? Get up."

His shoulders drop and his black Armani slacks move as comfortably as a new pair of fresh sweatpants as he walks toward the door.

"I knew the nigga I remembered in the institute was in there somewhere. You been out here too long if you think that soft shit was gonna work for me."

"Shortie, you ain't seen shit yet."

They didn't get halfway inside the elevator at the Super 8, off Indian Head Highway in Maryland, before he stuffs Yvonna with nine inches of dick. Grabbing her around her waist, he pulls her toward the back of the elevator and her body rests against his chest. To the naked eye they look like a loving couple. When two people get on from the next floor, and stand in front of them, they smile. The couple doesn't see her skirt hiked up, with his dick inside her.

"Bitch, I'm about to rip that pussy up when we get in that muthafucka," he whispers in her ear.

"Nigga, don't talk shit." She smiles when they look at them suspiciously. "Show and prove!"

She wouldn't dare tell him that he was already ripping her pussy up, due to his thickness. When the elevator opens, he pulls his dick out of her wet pussy, adjusts his pants, and straightens her skirt.

"Have fun," Yvonna tells the elevator couple.

He snatches her and the violence he is exhibiting is doing nothing but turning her on even more. Bradshaw is clearly the right man for the job; he reminds her of Bilal.

Once they get to the room, he opens the door and she walks in first. When the door closes, he smacks her so hard that for a moment she gets intimidated. She falls on the floor and feels the sting from her rug-burned, scratched-up knees. She rolls over and licks the blood from the corner of her mouth. Lying flat on her back, she wiggles out of the black skirt she's wearing.

"That's how the fuck I like it," she says. When

her skirt is off, she removes her panties and opens her legs wide. Then she spreads her soft pussy lips apart so that he can see her already wet pink center. "You made it slick. Now come get it."

"I got this shit." He takes his pants off. They drop to the floor and he removes his boxers. There, before her, stands not necessarily the longest but certainly the widest dick she's ever seen in her life. He strokes his already rock hardness in his hand. "I guess your husband ain't hittin' that thing right, after all."

"What husband, nigga?" she says as she moves around erotically.

"The husband you supposedly married." He gets down on the floor and is about to plunge into her. His muscles buckle as he prepares to dive into her.

"I ain't married. And even if I was, I wouldn't give a fuck right now."

He laughs at her defiance and eases into her slowly, before going deeper.

"*Awwwwww!* That's right, daddy! Now you hittin' that shit! How you know I like it like that, huh?"

"So you like cheatin' on your husband?" he asks. He has one hand on her throat and the other on the floor for support.

In her mind it is weird that he chooses to mention Dave. And for a second it turns her off. But she gets herself aroused again and moves into his sexual dives.

"Yeah, I'm cheatin' on his wack ass. And if you don't fuck me harder than this . . . you 'bout to get the fuck up."

He hits her again. *And again.* She is on the verge of cumming and is so aroused by his violence that she isn't going to be able to control her orgasm.

Feeling as if he is about to release, he places his fingers in her mouth and she slowly runs her tongue up and down his digits.

"Awww . . . fuuuuuuckkk!" he yells. "This shit too fuckin' good!"

"I'm cummin' too!" Her screams join his.

In seconds he releases himself into her and she gladly accepts. Afterward, he smiles at her, rubbing her cheek.

"You wild as shit," he tells her, looking into her eyes.

"Apparently not wilder than you," she says. Her face and body are a little sore from the violence.

He picks her up and places her gently on the bed. Then he places the covers over her partially nude body.

"You're different," she tells him as he scoots under the covers with her.

"Why's that?"

"One minute you're kickin' my ass, and the next minute you're caring about me."

"That's what you like, ain't it?"

She giggles and says, "What you think?"

"Okay . . . so I gave you what you wanted. Nothing more and nothing less."

She is silent before she says, "Am I going to see you again?"

"Now you wanna see a nigga again, huh? After he kick ya ass?"

"Yeah. I like a real nigga."

"I'm real, whether I hit you or not."

"That might be true, but you wouldn't be real enough for me."

"I wonder how *real* you really are?"

"You wanna find out?"

"Yeah. I got a promise I got to keep. You gonna help me?"

"Yes."

"You say yes before knowing what it is?"

"I trust you're not gonna give me nothin' I can't handle. And judgin' by the look in your eyes, I think I might like it."

Yvonna hops out of bed. Her ass jiggles a little, sending Bradshaw on another sexual frenzy. She picks up her purse from the floor and removes her phone. She is perfectly confident in her nakedness, and this is another attraction to him.

"Ming, meet me at the hotel I texted you earlier," she says, looking at him. "He's with it."

"Ming?" He smiles at the idea of having two women at the same time.

"Ming." She assures him with her eyes, already knowing he's in for a treat.

His eyes sparkle and he licks his lips. She is still smiling when she realizes Penny will be coming home soon. And if she doesn't hurry, it might be too late to prevent her from going downstairs. Although she doesn't peg her as the nosy type, she can't be sure. Penny's cell rings twice before she picks up.

"Hey, sweetheart. Are you okay?"

"Yeah, I'm good. I was wondering when you're going to be home from work. I was going to wait up for you."

"Awww, you so sweet. Sometimes I think I don't deserve ya!"

Yvonna laughs, until she sees Bradshaw in the bed, at full thickness again. Her pussy pulsates and she wants to jump on top of him for a ride. Ming, being only around the corner, knocks on the door. Bradshaw opens it, naked. The moment Ming steps inside, she drops the short red raincoat she's wearing and greets him with a kiss. All without saying even hello!

Bradshaw places his hand behind her head and kisses her back. The tattoo on Ming's back turns Yvonna on as she looks at the interaction between two strangers. Bradshaw picks Ming up and carries her to the bed. With her shoes still on, Ming hops on top of him and rides his dick, letting her head drop behind her. At this point Yvonna doesn't know what the fuck Penny's old ass is talking about on the phone.

"Get ova here," Bradshaw says to Yvonna as he pumps into Ming.

"Are ya there, baby?" Penny asks.

"Oh . . . uh . . . yeah."

"Oh, I thought I lost you. Did you hear what I said?"

"Fuck no," she blurts out.

"Yvonna?" Penny says her name, wondering if she is splitting personalities again. "Are you okay?"

Now Bradshaw has facilitated sixty-nine, and Yvonna's pussy is dripping wet. She doesn't know if she should join them or get her rocks off by watching.

"Yeah, I'm fine."

"Okay. Well, I'm not gonna make it home 'til five this mornin'. They asked old Penny to help out in the maternity unit. And we got some lady who's 'bout to pop any minute now."

"Aw . . . that's messed up," she says, trying to hide her excitement. She's taking note of how Ming has the entire shaft of his dick in her mouth—balls and all. "Well, wake me up when you get home."

"Naw. I want you to get your rest. Now, I left you the tea you like so much in that microwave oven. I tell you, I don't understand why you young kids be messin' wit them microwave things. Anyhow, alls you got to do is hit enter and drink ya tea. Okay, sweetie?"

"I will."

"Good, 'cause I—"

Yvonna hangs up in Penny's face before she can finish her sentence when she sees Bradshaw's toes curl. He's about to cum and she doesn't want to miss the fun.

They spend the next six months hooking up to fuck, suck, and beat the hell out of each other. They even establish an understanding, and Yvonna never minds Brad fucking Ming on the side, from time to time, as long as he breaks her off. Somehow, during these months, Yvonna grows closer to Penny too.

Yvonna's only problem with Penny is that she seems to flip out when Yvonna doesn't come straight home. And since that is about three times a week, they are often at odds. Still, Yvonna has to say, with her new man, and new best friend, she is having the time of her life.

There's No Pain Like Not Knowing

It is after midnight; and like he has every day for the past six months since his wife went missing, he roams around their home, waiting on word of her return. Still, he hears nothing. The lights flicker on and off and he looks up, thinking the bulbs need to be changed. He does nothing, because flickering lights are the least of his worries.

Guilt took him when she initially didn't come home. He wondered if his abuse caused her to leave. Then he grew angry. How dare she leave him? If their marriage failed, he would be the one to make the call that it was over—not her. When neither guilt nor anger made him feel better, he settled on the overwhelming sense of loss.

Deciding to check on their children, he walks

to their room and slowly opens their door. The light from the hallway shines against their small, sleeping faces without waking them. He smiles, leans up against the doorway, and stares. How he wishes he could close his eyes for one moment. Sleep deprivation has claimed him. And although he wants rest, his mind won't allow it.

He quietly closes the door and walks to the living room. Grabbing the Rémy bottle off the table, he pours a drink on the rocks.

"Where are you, Treyana? Where are you?" The full glass rests in his hand.

When she doesn't answer, he swallows the entire drink and pours another. He does this four times before the effects finally take hold of him.

He looks at the mail accumulating on the table. Treyana took care of the bills; so leaving them is his way of defying the obvious, that Treyana may never come home.

Under the mound of cards, circulars, and bills, he sees the edge of a red envelope. He pushes the others aside and examines the envelope fully. There is no return address and his name is written with penmanship so perfect that it looks like it isn't real. Curious, he opens it at once and pulls out a purple card with the same handwriting:

Losing a love brings a pain you can't deny.
But have you ever looked in your sons' eyes?
If you do, I'm sure you'll see.
The life you live is full of deceit.

HATE LIST 2: LOOSE CANNON

I'm sure you think I don't speak truth.
But a small blood test brings with it proof.

The note falls out of his hand and floats to the floor. His right leg shakes violently and he bears down on it with unusual force to get it to stop. Like the card said, he can't deny that his sons don't have his eyes. He never told Treyana how he felt, and he always blamed himself for being skeptical. But the years brought time; and still, they looked more and more unlike him. *Familiar,* no doubt, but unlike him.

Slowly he rises and walks back toward his children's room. And as if they know it is time for their mother's secret to be revealed, they stir in their beds and look at him in the doorway.

Tears roll down his eyes as he realizes that the children in the room, the ones he cared for all their lives, are not of his blood and not worthy of bearing his last name. Their eyes say it all. Sure, they are his wife's children, but he could not say with uncertainty that they are *his* sons. Now he needs answers more than anything, and he is willing to do what he has to do to get them.

Feels Too Good

Yvonna wakes up to a peaceful view of the morning sky from Bradshaw's bedroom window. The sun shines brightly and she smiles at its view. She is at peace. The heat from Bradshaw's body feels like a warm electric blanket against her bare skin. She has to give it to herself. . . . She always could pull a top-notch nigga, crazy or not.

When she backs up a little into Bradshaw, he pulls her closer. Her body has gotten fuller, and she has gone from a size six to twelve—although it seems to be all in the right places. Loving how his hands move over her body, she decides to turn around to get a better view of her man, although they haven't made it official.

When she turns around, she sees a leg draped over his waist with a red pump wiggling. Gabriella rises from behind him and rests her head on his shoulder. She smiles. Yvonna doesn't.

"You didn't think you could get rid of me, did you?" It has been weeks since Yvonna has seen her.

Yvonna hops out of bed and stares at the scene as if she's pushed into a horror movie. Missing the warmth of Yvonna's body, Brad opens his eyes and says, "What's wrong, shortie?" He looks behind him and back at her. "Everything okay?"

"Yeah, what's wrong, bitch? Tell this nigga yo ass certified so he can leave you like the rest of them. Go ahead!"

Yvonna looks at Gabriella instead of Bradshaw. And since she sees her resting on his arm, this is where her attention goes. To him it looks like she's looking at his shoulder.

"Yvonna! You a'ight?" he asks, sitting up. Gabriella stands up, and Yvonna sees her wearing a red bra-and-panty set.

"The man is talking to you, and here you are staring into space like a dumb ass." Gabriella places her hands on her hips.

"It's happening again?" Bradshaw asks. For the first time since she sees Gabriella in the room, she acknowledges him by looking into his eyes. "You wanna talk about it, baby?"

A tear runs down her face. "I just want this to stop. I don't want to be like this."

"Then make it stop. Take the medicine they give you."

"You don't understand. I'm scared."

"Scared of what? Of makin' this shit stop?"

"No. Of being alone. I'm scared that I won't be strong enough without her." She looks at him with pleading eyes.

"You are strong enough. She is *you*."

Bradshaw stands up and walks toward her. She has forgotten that with him she doesn't have to lie. They had been in the mental institution together. And because she could be herself with him, this makes her more vulnerable to heartache. And vulnerability is the one emotion she tries to block by protecting herself through creating the Gabriella personality. Bradshaw pulls Yvonna into his chest and holds her strongly.

"I got you, Yvonna. You better than this shit. You been through this already and you came through. You are strong."

Yvonna tries to listen, but all she can think about is that once he releases her, Gabriella will be there still, and he'd be wrong. She needs him to be right. She needs to trust someone. Bradshaw is the kind of man she needs. He is strong . . . kinky . . . and willing to stick by her, despite her disorder.

"You stupid if you fall in love with this nigga! You know the games men play!"

Yvonna sobs harder and Bradshaw holds her tighter, rocking her in his arms. "You bigger than this shit! You can control it, Yvonna. Stay with me. Tell me you bigger! Tell me!"

"I can't."

"Yes, you can! You control this shit, not the other way around! Now let me hear you say it, baby! Let me hear you be what I know you can. Will this shit!"

He maintains the hold he has on her, until the words he needs to hear exit her soft lips.

"I . . . uh . . . am stronger . . . than this," she says in a low voice.

"I can't hear you! The woman I met got this shit under control. Now say it again. And when I let you go, she gonna be gone. Okay?" Yvonna doesn't respond and he grips her arms tighter, altering the ease of the blood flowing through her arms. With stern eyes focused on her, he says, "Do you hear me?"

"Y-yes."

Bradshaw takes his hands off her and backs up slowly. Her view is partially blocked because of his muscular chest and broad shoulders. The farther he steps back, the better her view becomes—until, finally, she can confirm that there are no signs of Gabriella.

"She here?" he asks hopefully.

"No," she says, looking behind her and around the room. "She's not here."

In this moment she isn't the tough girl she usually is. But out of the darkness, she gains light. Bradshaw is right. She went against everything she knows and trusted him, and he is right.

He smiles. "See, you got this shit."

She's falling for him, and she decides to talk to

him seriously about her disorder. She wants to be open about everything before putting the rest of her heart into him. Because history has shown that love is not her friend—and unless he is Father Time—she doesn't see how now would be any different. The vibration of her phone in her purse breaks her attention. She walks toward it and picks it up. Bradshaw jumps back in bed.

"Who is it?"

"Penny. She callin' from the house."

"Why so many times?"

"I don't know."

She presses ignore. And with the screen clear, she's able to scroll through twenty missed calls from Penny. It makes no sense. Has she found Treyana in the basement of her home? One thing is certain—she can't wait around here to find out.

I'm Not Trying to Be

Yvonna creeps up the steps of Penny's home carefully. She wants to avoid her until she finds out how much she knows. She loves Penny. In fact, they spend many days together, talking about Penny's life and the details Yvonna feels comfortable sharing about her past. Penny is quickly becoming the mother Yvonna always wanted, despite not bearing one physical resemblance. But when it comes to her privacy—and the protection of it—Yvonna doesn't fuck around.

Fuck does this greasy black bitch want, anyway? she thinks. *Calling my phone like she lost her mind!*

After peeking into the front window briefly, she decides to go inside when she doesn't see her anywhere. It is important that Yvonna remains as silent as possible. Once inside, she looks around again.

Penny, please don't say you went downstairs after I asked you not to, she silently implores. *Please. I don't want to hurt you.*

She moves cautiously toward the basement. Once she arrives at the basement door, she removes the small key to unlock it. She opens the door and is about to go downstairs, when she sees Penny in the kitchen. She is so preoccupied with chopping a small object that she doesn't notice Yvonna about ten feet away from her.

Taking one more step, Yvonna can see the object is a pill. *What are you doing?* she thinks. When the item is small enough, Penny scoops it off the counter with her hand and dusts it into the teacup that Yvonna uses regularly. Yvonna's mouth drops open. *You wretched bitch!* When the powder is within the cup, Penny stirs the potion.

Yvonna is conflicted. The tea Penny told her was made with love was made with poison. Not wanting Penny to know she is onto her black ass, she backs up carefully and makes her way to the basement. She is hurt and tears roll down her face. She loves Penny, and here she is betraying her. She'd deal with her later, and in her own way. For sure.

"When are you going to let me go? I been here for months," Treyana asks as she sits on the floor with her arms tied behind her back. She is leaning against an old radiator and is wearing a red shirt;

otherwise, she is naked from the waist down. Her hair is all over her head and she looks like the dusty bitch she was before Yvonna cleaned her up years earlier. "My husband is going to come looking for me. Please let me go."

"I can't do that, so don't ask me, sweetheart." Yvonna stands over her and looks down at her. "And don't worry about your husband coming for you. I sent him a little message on your behalf. If anything, you'll be lucky if he doesn't come through that door and help me kill you. Seeing as though you cheated on him with my dead boyfriend, and all. It seems Bilal had a thing for nasty bitches."

"What did you tell Avante?" Treyana tries to sit up straight.

"I told him to look into the eyes of his children." Yvonna sits on her bed. "I'm sure he'll realize after reading it that they look nothing like him. He probably already knows. I can't even believe I missed it."

Treyana's head drops. "Why are you doing this to me? And to my family? Why don't you just leave us alone?"

"Because I warned you about messing with me, and you didn't listen."

She is quiet before saying, "You're so unhappy you don't even realize it. But I know one day, things are going to change for you. And when they do, they're going to be for the worse. One day you'll get exactly what you deserve."

"I have no doubt I will. But . . . you're first."

Yvonna changes into her comfortable clothing and walks back upstairs, locking the door behind her. She must deal with Penny, and her actions will depend on Penny's response.

"Yvonna, how are you, sweetheart?"

Yvonna sits on the couch, angry with Penny for putting her in this situation. "I'm fine."

Penny places a hot cup of tea next to her. "That's good, sweetheart. 'Cause when I knocked on your door, and you ain't ansa this morning, old Penny got worried."

"And why would *old-ass Penny* worry and call my phone twenty million times?"

"I wasn't trying to be a bother. Just worried about you, that's all."

Yvonna lifts the tea and holds it to her mouth, like she is about to drink it. She sees Penny's bushy eyebrows rise in the hope that she'll down the poison, so Yvonna decides to fuck with her a little bit.

"So you worry about me, huh?" She places the cup down, and Penny's breath releases from her body in disappointment. She wants Yvonna to drink the tea so badly that it's showing in her actions.

"Drink your tea, baby. It's good for you."

"I will. But what's wrong? Are you okay?"

"Oh . . . uh . . . yes, I am."

"You don't look it. Have some tea."

"I can't!" Penny yells, standing up.

"Why not? I'll just make myself another cup."

"That's okay. I'll make some later."

"If you let this bitch get by without handling her, I'm gonna take care of her myself tonight."

Yvonna tries to ignore Gabriella's voice. And because it is more difficult now to block her out than it was the night before, she is starting to realize that the medicine Penny gave her might have been working. She wonders how long she's been giving it to her. It is also evident that without it she becomes more emotionally volatile, causing the Gabriella personality to take over totally.

"I know you hear me, Yvonna. Don't fuck wit me! I'm not going to allow you to ignore me much longer. I'm the only one who cares about you."

"Are you okay?" Penny asks, witnessing the blank expression on Yvonna's face. "You don't look too good, chile."

"Yvonna, kill this bitch right now! She been druggin' you, and you gonna let her get away with it?"

Trying to protect Penny, Yvonna gets up from the sofa and moves hurriedly toward the basement.

"Yvonna, are you okay?" Penny asks, walking behind her.

Silence.

"Yvonna . . . talk to me."

Yvonna feels around in her pockets for the key to unlock the door. She is nervous and sweat begins to form on her forehead. She has to get away. If she doesn't, she will most certainly hurt Penny.

"Yvonna, you don't have to do this. You don't have to deal wit this kinda pressha alone. I'm here for you. But you got to let me do for you what I can."

"Kill her, Yvonna! Kill her now! She's violating. She's into our space! Take care of her! I don't trust her!"

"Baby," Penny says, touching her shoulder.

Yvonna grabs Penny's hand and squeezes it so hard that her knuckles sound as if they are about to crack.

"Keep your hands off me, bitch," she tells her before opening the door and closing the door behind her. "Stay the fuck away from me!" she shouts.

When Yvonna makes it downstairs, she muscles up for another problem when she doesn't see Treyana tied against the rusted radiator anymore. Panic immediately sets in and she hustles toward the back of the basement, toward the back entrance.

"Where are you, bitch?" she asks, looking everywhere.

Silence.

"I know you in here somewhere. If I have to come get you, I'm not going to be nice. I'm serious. Don't fuck with me."

Yvonna picks up the rusted weed clippers from a worktable and walks softly toward the back door. Once at the door, she sees the red shirt. Treyana is on the floor crawling, until Yvonna grabs her back

into the house. Closing the door, she locks it behind her.

"You thought you were gonna get away from me
that easy?" she asks, pulling her hair.

"Let me go! I wanna see my kids. I miss my
family!"

"You gonna miss more than that! I told you I
couldn't let you go until my plan was done. But
you just had to be a busybody, bitch. Now you're
going to pay big-time for this shit! You hear me?"

Treyana turns around, kicking and swinging
wildly. She stands up and is about to run when
Yvonna runs after her. The edge of a metal worktable digs into her stomach because Treyana is not
in her grip. When Treyana stumbles and falls,
Yvonna dives after her. Then she grabs her right
hand and jabs the clippers into her fingers, over
and over again.

"*Awwwwww!* You're hurting me! Please stop!
Somebody help me!"

Boom! Boom! Boom!

Penny hears the commotion from upstairs and
bangs on the door with the force of six men. *Still*,
the reinforced door she had built about five years
earlier doesn't budge. She made it secure in case
she ever had to live there for shelter in an emer-
gency situation. Now she wishes she hadn't.

"Now you did it! Now I'm gonna fuck you up
for this!"

Yvonna digs the weed clippers deeper into Treyana's hand. Blood splatters everywhere, and all kinds of thoughts enter her mind. What is she going to do with her now? How is she going to explain to Penny where the commotion came from? And most of all, how is she going to dispose of the body?

After the fifth stab Treyana appears to be going out of consciousness; and for some reason Yvonna is growing weaker too. Perhaps it was all the energy she exerted in restraining and assaulting her.

No . . . something else is definitely going on. Treyana passes out, and Yvonna is suddenly consumed with pain. She believes Treyana must've stabbed her and she didn't realize it.

"What did you do to me?" Yvonna asks weakly.

Right before she gets her answer, Penny kicks in the back door and sees Yvonna lying in a puddle of her own blood, with her fingers mutilated. And most important, she is all *alone*.

A Packed Decision

The cafeteria at FCI Fairton is crowded with hungry inmates. Everybody is either talking about the jail time they had left, or what they will do as free men. Tree sits at the table with four others, while Swoopes talks about his life prior to being incarcerated.

Tree knows Swoopes from the past, but Swoopes doesn't recognize him. Tree is glad he doesn't. Their past is not worth remembering, and it wouldn't prevent Tree from doing what needs to be done. At first, he wasn't going to carry out his part of the deal, even after Yvonna murdered the correctional officer. But after she murdered Bernice, he knew that not following through on the plan would cause him more problems than one body was worth. Especially after learning that the woman he had initially thought was Treyana is *actually* Yvonna Harris, the woman he'd read about in the paper years earlier.

The discovery came while looking at some old photos Swoopes had in his room of Bilal and his friends. Although Swoopes was not happy about her being in any of his photos, he didn't trash them, because a few of those pictures were taken during parties he wanted to remember.

It was easy for Tree to be fooled by Yvonna's disguise, because she always wore a wig in the pictures she sent. But what Yvonna didn't know was that he was also familiar with her.

"Yo, Swoopes, tell me about that crazy bitch you were talking about again."

"Who? Yvonna?" he asks. His left eye is still covered by a black eye patch, and his right hand is missing the three fingers that the men he owed money to chopped off for a debt he paid late.

"Yeah. You neva got through tellin' me, 'cause that bitch-ass nigga Jake started talkin' 'bout that broad, and shit."

"Oh yeah," he says, remembering their conversation in the TV room earlier. "So, look, this bitch was crazy as shit. She was slicin' niggas' dicks off, cuttin' up people's kids, and rapin' other girls, and shit." He is lying.

"Man, how the fuck did she do all that and it took them all that time to catch her?"

"You actin' like the police are smart or somethin'. It's easy to get ova on them muthafuckas."

"Well, if it's so easy, how come you in here?"
"Corn," another inmate, asks after laughing. Inmates at the table chuckle at this. Corn has huge arms and large knuckles, but most inmates think his bark is worse than his bite. He sees Swoopes's eye patch and missing fingers as weaknesses.

"Dis nigga crazy," he responds, pointing at him while looking at Tree. "First off, do you even know me?" The question is rhetorical, because he knows he doesn't. "I didn't think so, so stay the fuck out of my business."

"I don't need to know you. If you talkin' at the table, you talkin' to everybody." Corn cracks his knuckles and looks at him. He is clearly mad about something and has decided to take it out on who he perceives to be the weakest man in the room.

Swoopes gives him a once over and ignores him. This embarrasses Corn and induces a surge of anger through his body.

"And like I said, before I was interrupted by this sucka-ass nigga, this broad runnin' around the city merkin' niggas left and right. I think some of the cops knew and was lettin' her get away wit that shit."

As Swoopes continues with his conversation, Corn is breathing in and out heavily. He is building himself up to take some kind of action.

"She killed 'bout two of the niggas I used to roll wit . . ." Swoopes is in midsentence when Corn takes his milk carton and smacks it up against his face. *Splash!*

Swoopes's patch moves and exposes his damaged eye. He moves it back in place and hits him with blow after blow. Corn quickly finds out that Swoopes's handicap is not a handicap, after all. Finally, with one last blow, Corn is knocked to the floor. His legs fly up in the air and his black boot comes off his foot, smacking him in the face. Niggas are heckling his ass and making the situation worse.

"Damn, that nigga fuckin' his shit up!" someone yells.

"Dude ain't got one in since he smacked him in the face with the carton."

The COs don't see what is going on because their attention is drawn to another argument that happens across the way. Swoopes is just about to punish Corn's ass for more points, until he sees two inmates rush toward him. Tree decides to give him a hand when he hits the first dude up to bat, fracturing his nose on impact.

When "Babble Mouth" Johnson, a snitching-ass white inmate, decides to increase his kiss-ass points by alerting the COs of the fight, Swoopes and Tree take their seats. Everyone at the table sits down to avoid being pointed out and asked to give an account of what happened. Swoopes grabs his food and acts natural, while Tree tosses his meal around in his tray. The inmates look like a well-behaved group of punk bitches.

"What happened?" an officer asks Tree.

"I don't know," Tree tells him, swallowing his food. "You gotta ask them niggas down there."

"What happened, Roberts?" he asks Corn, who is now on his feet.

He wipes the blood off the corner of his mouth, grabs his boot, and looks at Swoopes. "Nothin'. I fell."

"You fell, huh?" he asks, with an inquisitor's glare. He nods. "Well, fall your ass out of here before you get locked down."

Corn walks away, but not without looking at Swoopes and Tree again. The COs look at everyone at the table and follow Corn away from the scene. When they are gone, Swoopes and Tree laugh.

"Fuck was wrong wit that nigga?"

"He mad 'cause that bitch he dealin' wit fuckin' wit his roommate. He took pictures of that nigga's girl and her address and started writing her. That slut wrote back."

"Are you serious?"

"Fuck yeah! She used to visit Corn, and his roommate would find somebody to see him on the same day. The whole time they'd be in each otha's face, and shit."

"Conversatin'?"

"Naw, just lookin' at each otha across the room, and shit. But a week later the broad sends a letter and forgets who she was sendin' it to. She meant to send it to his roommate, but Corn got it, instead, and flipped. They locked his ass down for ninety days because he went crazy. Tearin' shit down in his room." Tree laughs. "He did all that shit, and that nigga that took his bitch was right in his cell with him. They said this nigga was cryin' and askin' him why he broke his heart." Everyone chuckles. "I'm surprised you ain't hear that shit."

"Man, I neva even looked at that nigga in my life."

"I feel you. But, anyway, his roommate got out a day later. He went on parole, and my man, Shawn D from Northwest, said he moved in wit that bitch and they gettin' married."

"Damn . . . that's some foul shit!"

"That's how niggas be. You gotta watch what's yours."

"On that note I'm out. I got some shit to take care of back in the cell." Swoopes gives Tree a pound. "One."

"One," Tree responds.

When he leaves, Stevie, who is sitting right next to him, as if they aren't in cahoots, speaks through tightened lips.

"So when you want me to do that?" he asks, grabbing a milk carton to cover his lips.

"Tonight. His celly in the infirmary, so he'll be by himself."

Stevie grabs his dick, just thinking about fucking Swoopes. Unlike other down-low brothers, he admits to fucking other men. And if somebody challenges him on it, he has no problems standing up for what he believes in. And in this case he believes in tight-ass buttholes.

"Cool. Don't worry. I got that shit. I'll take the smokes, but I'da did it for free."

Tree is silent, because Stevie is talking too much.

"You neva did tell me why you want me to do this, though."

" 'Cause it's none of your business. Just remember the plan."

"Trust me. It will be my pleasure."

Swoopes is in his room, doing push-ups, with his head away from the door. He is just about to do his last set, when someone enters.

"Not now, Jo. I'm not done," he says, preparing to finish his exercise.

He thinks it is Jo Cramer coming for the tenth time that day to borrow his magazines. He is about to cuss his pressed ass out; but he doesn't get the chance to, when he feels the body weight of another man against his back. His face is smashed against the grungy, cold floor. And when he tries to speak, his tooth breaks and lodges underneath his tongue. The harder he fights, the more pressure is placed on top of him. His voice cannot rise because a large, callous hand is placed against his lips. This is the worst thing that could've happened to him.

When Swoopes was younger, his father, who was part of an underground child-sex ring, used to make him give oral sex every night after his wife, Bernice, went to bed. Bernice had married him when she left her ex-boyfriend Dylan during one of their fights. She was initially attracted to him because of how well she thought he took care of his adopted son. It didn't take her long to realize that what she believed was a lie. And truthfully, Bernice didn't know a lot about Poris or Dylan, for that matter.

Poris Mitchell, Swoopes's father, was a tall man, with very light skin. He wasn't very attractive; had it not been for his large home and money, and her need to make Dylan jealous, Bernice would have never dealt with him. A major characteristic about him was that whenever he showed emotion of any kind, his face would flush red.

It wasn't until his father tried to sexually abuse Bilal, Swoopes's stepbrother, that things changed in his life. To this day, Swoopes has nightmares; and it has impacted his relationships with men and women.

"Hi, boys. I just came to bring y'all some cookies and milk," Poris said after he entered the boys' bedroom.

"Where's my mother?" Bilal asked. His eyes lit up, but he knew eating food in the bed went against his mother's rules.

"She's asleep. Who wants chocolate chip, and who wants raisin?"

Taylor Mitchell sat on his bed with the covers raised

over his mouth, barely showing his eyes. He saw his father's complexion and knew what he really wanted. Sex.

"I'll take chocolate!" Bilal, who was only ten at the time, yelled. Poris smiled, having won him over, and sat on the edge of his bed.

"What about you, son? You want oatmeal raisin or chocolate?"

"I don't want any." He shook his head repeatedly.

"You sure? They're really good."

"I'm sure."

"Yes, you do. Why don't you come on over here and sit next to me and Bilal."

"Daddy, I don't want to."

"Taylor Mitchell, you get over here this instant!" he demanded.

Feeling uncomfortable with Poris's change of attitude, Bilal decided to defend his stepbrother.

"On second thought, I don't want any cookies."

Poris whipped his head around and looked at Bilal.

"Yes, you do," he told him, with a treacherous stare. "And so you don't get any cookies on your pajamas, why don't you take off your shirt. You don't want me to tell your mother you're eating in the bed, do you?"

Bilal, who was still young and confused, did as he was told. And before long, Taylor sat on the edge of the bed next to them.

"Look at you," Poris said to Bilal in a caring tone. "You have such a beautiful chest. Doesn't he have a beautiful chest, Taylor?" Taylor couldn't face Bilal. He was unnerved. "Don't be rude! Look at him, Taylor!"

Taylor raised his eyes a little and saw the confusion on Bilal's face.

"What's going on?" Bilal asked.

"Nothin'. We're all friends here and we like to touch one another," Poris said after placing his hand on his immature chest. "Touch your brother, Taylor."

"No . . . please," he said, shaking his head. "I don't want to."

"Do it!"

Bilal finally saw what was happening. His mother warned him of freak-ass niggas like this. Most important, she told him what to do if something like this ever happened. And he remembered everything she said.

"I'm gonna tell my mother!" he yelled in a strong, firm voice. "Don't put your fuckin' hands on me!"

For the first time Taylor raised his head and kept his eyes on Bilal. After Bilal challenged him, he ran out of the room toward Poris and Bernice's bedroom. When she found out what had happened, she felt helpless and hurt that she had placed her only son in so much danger. Immediately she got on the phone and called the police. Afterward, she made mental notes to divorce her husband of five months and take a heap of his money with her.

When the cops arrived that night, they asked Taylor if what Bilal was saying was true. Poris, who stood out of view of everyone else in the living room, gave Taylor a dark stare. He told him many times before that if he ever told anybody about what he made him do sexually, he'd kill him. But something about Bilal's strength made him strong and he wasn't as afraid as he usually was.

"Well, son? Is what your brother saying true or not?"

"Yes, it is."

Poris was locked up for child molestation, and Taylor was placed in foster home after foster home. He ran away so much, stealing people's possessions in the process, that he earned the nickname of "Swoopes." It would take him only a minute to swoop your shit right out from up under you.

The system, and life, had turned him into a cold, selfish person. Eventually Swoopes ran into Bilal many years later. Bilal was with the Young Black Millionarz. And after running away from people he owed money, Swoopes sought refuge with his stepbrother by joining the same YBM gang.

Bilal never told any of their mutual friends how Poris tried to violate both of them. Anyway, the topic was too embarrassing. But Swoopes always thought he had. He always felt like someone was judging him or wanted something from him.

What Swoopes didn't know was that he was onto something. Because although Bilal didn't tell any of their mutual friends their secret, he did tell the bitch he hated most of all, Yvonna. And when it was time, she decided to use his deep, dark secret against him.

The man moans deeply in Swoopes's ear as he takes his self-respect. Swoopes thinks he is about to die when he feels another man's penis being rammed in and out of him. For five minutes he is put into the worst physical and emotional pain of his entire life. And when the rape is over, he is hit with one swift motion on his right temple, rendering him unconscious.

"Where you goin', man?" Stevie asks, passing Tree in the hallway.

" 'Bout to go to sleep. I'ma get up wit you later."

"A'ight. I wanted to rap to you about that. Can we talk now? It's important."

Tree looks at him and says in a deep voice, "I said, *lada*, nigga."

Stevie walks away, confused at his response.

Once Tree arrives in his room, he rushes to the sink. Looking behind him once, to be sure no one is coming into his cell, he takes a cloth and wipes his soiled penis, mixed with semen and shit, as best he can. He decided to do the honor of raping Swoopes himself. It wasn't like he didn't have experience.

Taking one look at himself in the mirror, he's disgusted. Tree has been a closeted homosexual all his life. When his best friend was alive, they shared their compulsion together. Sometimes he missed Dylan, Bernice's ex-boyfriend . . . *and* his lover.

A New Chapter,
A New Story

"So how is she? I mean . . . has she regained her con-chus-ness?"

"Penny, you know I'm not supposed to be talking to you about a patient's case."

Penny stares at Yvonna wearily. Lately she hadn't been home; and when she did come back, she was hurt. "I know, Docta. But you see, I'm the only family she got."

Penny looks down at Yvonna, who is in bed, connected to several monitors and machines.

"Penny, you are not related to her. So why the interference?"

" 'Cause she needs me. Everybody needs somebody."

"Oh well," he says after a heavy breath. "Have it your way." Penny smiles. "I still don't understand how her fingers got mutilated, though. It doesn't make much sense."

"Like I said, someone was tryin' to break in my home and she fought 'em and they stabbed her. I caught 'em runnin' away."

Dr. June looks at her over his red-rimmed glasses. "You're lying, but there's nothing I can do. For your sake I hope you know what you're doing."

Before he leaves, she says, "Docta, do you think it's possible to ever fully get over multiple personality disorder? Not that she is havin' a problem. I just wanna know."

"Why?"

"Just curious, Docta. Really."

"Well, for starters it's not called 'multiple personality disorder' anymore. It's referred to as 'dissociative identity disorder,' or 'DID.' Usually the ego or personality will take control of the individual's behavior, which results in memory loss. Now, if I remember her case correctly, Yvonna not only experienced routine takeovers by other personalities, but she also was able to talk to and see them."

"I'm not talkin' 'bout her," Penny corrects him. "This is *just* a general question."

"Well, it's an odd general question."

"It's general, all the same."

He clears his throat and says, "Normally, only auditory hallucinations exist. And because of these vast differences, Yvonna's case, even though we aren't referring to her, is different."

"But can DID be cured?"

"Not unless they're able to reconnect the identities to make them one functioning individual."

"Thank you, Docta."

"Good luck, Penny."

When he leaves the room, she looks down at Yvonna's soft face. Penny had been placing antidepressants in her tea faithfully. She was aware that when Yvonna didn't come home, missing dosages could cause the disorder to resurface. That's why she lied to the authorities and the hospital staff about what had happened to her fingers. She didn't know what caused her to hurt herself, but she had a feeling DID was to blame.

"Get well, honey. I love you."

With that, she rubs her rough hand slowly across Yvonna's forehead and walks out of the room. And when she does, her eyes open. But Yvonna is not the same.

Introducing Gabriella,
the craziest bitch alive

Now Shyt Has Gotten Serious

The beeping of the monitors and the fashionless white robes were making her sick. She needed out. She needed to get away. And most of all . . . she needed revenge. But when Yvonna opens her eyes, she isn't herself. She is Gabriella—the dominant, the heartless, and the cruelest soul on the planet.

Yvonna duplicated personalities in an attempt to make the people in her life do, think, and act the way she thought they should be. This was why she'd often hold on to other personalities, like her father and then Treyana long after their deaths. Yvonna was the ruthless, and Gabriella was the heartless.

Gabriella committed the murders when Yvonna lost control of people and situations, although most of the time the murders occurred without Yvonna's recollection. But when Yvonna regained consciousness and identified with their personalities, despite them being dead, she was usually in control. Before long, violence becomes second nature.

Sure, she had other personalities prior to Gabriella. But when she came along, she forgot about them all. In fact, it was during the most confusing times of her life that Gabriella came to her.

"Yvonna, what are you doing up here?"

Yvonna sat on a worn-out blue recliner in the corner of her dark living room, looking out a window. She loved staring at the huge letter T *as she thought of another place, far, far away. She imagined she had loving parents and that they would somehow come back to take her away from a fucked-up reality, but these make-believe parents never came.*

"I wanna stay up here." Yvonna looked at her with the pleading eyes of a child. Her red dress was too small for her, and the red strawberries that were on the front of it were missing thread and lacking color. "I don't want to go downstairs."

"Well, you have to." Diana's tall, lanky body looked worn-out and abused. The dirty jeans that she wore were so thin in the knee and buttock areas that they were developing holes. And her large, tough black wig made her look much older than thirty-five. Still, there was beauty

on her caramel-colored face, but not in her eyes. "You're being rude to your father and his company. They love to see you dance, and they have guests."

"Mama, please. They don't make me dance. They make me—" Yvonna was cut off in midsentence by her mother's boisterous tone.

"Stop lyin' to me! Your father loves you! Now get downstairs!"

"But I'm scared, Mama. I don't like it down there. They hurt me."

"Yvonna Harris, get down them fuckin' stairs now!" When Yvonna didn't move, her mother grabbed her fragile shoulders roughly, meshing them together in an awkward motion. "You messin' shit up for me! Them men pay good money to see you dance. Besides, there are other kids down there. Don't you want to be with other kids?"

"No, Mama, I want to stay here with you." She held on to Diana's leg and she kicked her off. This was the most rebellious Yvonna had ever been.

"If I have to tell you again, you won't eat for a whole week! Now go!"

She released Yvonna. She was supposed to be her protector, yet she was the furthest thing from it. Diana couldn't safeguard anyone if she wanted to, because she was the keeper of many secrets.

"Okay, Mama, I'm going." She backed away from her.

"Good. And when you get back, I'll let you eat the cereal you like to eat for dinner. Okay?"

Yvonna nodded her head and walked to the basement. Her body trembled because she knew they'd be waiting.

They *always were, and there were* always *new ones. They were united by their sins. Once a month they'd come with their liquor, loud mouths, and video cameras to abuse children; and Yvonna's parents hosted the event, but why?*

Although she remembered most of the predators' faces prior to splitting into the Gabriella personality, after some time she forgot most of them. Instead of dwelling on such despair, she created Charmaine and Shelby to keep her company. Charmaine was the first personality she ever had, and Shelby followed sometime after that. They were with her during the worst years of abuse. The personalities, although distinct in their appearances, appeared to come from nowhere.

Yvonna bended the corner in the basement and looked at the five men present.

"What took you so long?" one asked.

"Yeah, you had us waiting," another one said.

Their eyes followed her, until she stood before them while Yvonna's father sat on the chair and looked at her with lust. The strangers were seated in a circle, with three naked young boys standing in the middle. Joe and Diana were respected in their group because of their access to children. No one asked where they got the children from, and no one cared.

The five men present were Joe Harris, Dylan Merrick,

Tamal "Tree" Green, Poris Mitchell, and Derrick Knight. And they all had three things in common: They all enjoyed having sex with young children. They all paid for it. They all deserved to burn in hell. It was Dylan and Tamal's first time attending, but it wouldn't be their last. It took the seemingly bisexual couple forever to win Joe and Diana's trust, and their hard work had finally paid off.

"You hear them, girl?" Joe continued. "What took you so long?"

"I was talking to Mama. Upstairs," she said in a weak voice.

"Don't be sorry, get over here."

Yvonna walked slowly in the middle, and suddenly she saw Charmaine and Shelby in a corner. Although most of the men preferred boys, Tamal and Dylan seemed to like both. They were the ones who requested Yvonna.

"Get on top of her," Tamal told one of the young boys once she was in the middle. Her red dress sat at her feet. "And put your mouth on her young pussy. She like that. Don't you, Yvonna?"

Yvonna started to cry, and her personalities, Charmaine and Shelby, began shaking in the corner. They were duplicates of her current mental state: innocent, young, and helpless.

"Na-na-now, I like that," Tree said, looking at the boy stoop down. He had a weird speech impediment when it came to saying the word "now." He would stutter a few times before getting the word out.

"Please," Yvonna sobbed. "I don't like this."

"Shut up! You do like it, you young bitch!" Joe said. He got up and smacked her in the face. "Stop acting like you don't!"

"Man, I paid my money to see this," Dylan disputed. "If she don't do it, I'ma take my money elsewhere."

"She gonna do it." Tamal stopped him. "Ain't you?"

Dylan wasn't that into women. In fact, the only woman he ever cared about was Bernice, and that was only because she bore him a son. Their heterosexual relationship concealed his sexuality. At first, he had thoughts of sexually abusing Bilal; he even grew excited the closer the day came to his birth. But when his son was born and he looked into his eyes, Dylan realized he couldn't bring himself to do it. He decided to stick to abusing other people's children. Not feeling totally satisfied behind closed doors, he managed to create a new fantasy with Bernice.

It consisted of placing foreign objects in and out of his ass. Although it soothed some of his urges, it wasn't until he met Tamal "Tree" Green that he was totally complete. With Tamal, he could play the closeted homosexual game. This worked for a while, until Tamal wanted something Dylan wasn't able to give him—a public gay relationship. This enraged Tamal, who wanted Dylan to leave Bernice. So, naturally, when Bernice, who knew nothing about her boyfriend's sexuality, approached Tree with an idea to make some money, he accepted in the name of revenge.

Realizing pleading with the adults would not stop anything from happening, Yvonna complied and endured the sexual abuse as they coached the children along.

"Charmaine and Shelby, please," she begged during the violation of her body. "Help me."

"Who you talking to?" Derrick, a short man who was abused himself as a child, asked. "Why are you always talking to yourself?"

"Please, Charmaine and Shelby, help me."

They didn't help her, because they couldn't. They cowered in the corner and turned their backs on her. And after fifteen minutes of abuse and taping, the men tired of her.

"Now you can leave," Joe told her. "Come, give Daddy a kiss first."

She did as she was told and looked back at the boys, feeling sorrow for them. One of the children was Taylor Mitchell. He kept his head down and covered his privates with his hands. He seemed detached and angry. Yvonna grabbed her dress and looked at Charmaine and Shelby once more. She felt they left her dejected and all alone; and before long she hated them.

With her clothing partially on, Yvonna ran back up the stairs, broken inside. Right before she took solace in her bedroom, she saw her mother sitting in the recliner with a new child in her arms. Jhane, the woman she'd grown to know as her aunt, was standing above Diana. Her face had traces of dried tears upon it. She was thin and the years of drug abuse had taken its toll on her body. When Yvonna looked at Jhane, a woman she saw no more than three times, Jhane turned away from her.

And for some reason, Yvonna longed to have a relationship with her. It never happened.

Diana handed Jhane some money; and after tucking it in her worn-out jean pocket, Yvonna watched her leave. Once she was gone, Diana rocked the baby lovingly in her arms. Yvonna would have given anything for her mother to hold her with such care.

"Who is that?" Yvonna asked in a soft tone.

"Why?"

"Just wanna know," she said, walking closer.

"Did you finish dancing for the men downstairs?"

Yvonna's mother always referred to what went on downstairs as "dancing," and Yvonna wondered if she really *knew* what they were doing to her.

"Yes, Mama, I did. Who's that?" she repeated.

Diana's eyes look at the ceiling as she thought of a lie. When she found an appropriate answer, she said, "Stop being dumb. You know this is your baby sister."

"Baby sister?" Yvonna asked, focusing on the baby's features. She'd been living there alone with her mother and father and never had a sister. "But I don't have a sister."

Diana gripped her up by her dress again with one hand and yelled, "You betta not *eva* tell nobody that shit! If you do, I'll give you away."

Yvonna didn't have a great life, anyway, but she certainly didn't want to go somewhere that could be worse.

"You do have a baby sister! Do you hear me?" Diana's breasts pressed against the baby's small head, and Yvonna was worried she'd smother her.

"Yes. Yes . . . I know, Mama." She looked back with concern at the baby.

Diana let Yvonna go and focused, instead, on the child in her arms.

"That's right. Now, if anybody asks you, her name is Jesse. Jesse is gonna make me a lot of money."

"Okay, Mama."

"What's her name, Yvonna?" she asked, giving her an on-the-spot test.

"Jesse. Jesse Harris."

"Now get out of my face and wash up. You stink."

Yvonna didn't realize, but in that moment something changed inside her. She'd developed a strength she never knew existed. And, most of all, she developed a strong unconditional love for another. She made up her mind that she'd always protect her, even if her life depended on it. Yvonna did not want the same dangers to come to baby Jesse that she had endured.

In her room she was still thinking about baby Jesse when she saw someone inside.

"Who are you?" she said loudly. The girl had startled her.

"Yvonna, are you talkin' to yourself again?"

Yvonna, who knew she'd suffer a severe beating if she was caught talking to herself, began to tremble. "No, Mama! I'm not talking to myself."

"Good! Now take a bath and clean that room!"

Yvonna breathed a little easier and closed the door.

"How did you get in here?"

"I let myself in. You don't remember me? I'm your new best friend."

"But I don't have a best friend."

"Yes, you do. Do you wanna be friends with me?" She seemed confident, and Yvonna wished she were the same way.

"What's your name?" she asked.

"Gabriella." She smiled. "And don't worry 'bout nothin'. I'm going to protect you from now on. Whenever you're sad, or hurt, I'll be by your side. Forever and ever. *"*

Yvonna developed Gabriella to protect her baby sister. And although Shelby and Charmaine would show up every now and again, it was Gabriella she favored. Before long the others were completely gone.

Gabriella opens her eyes in her hospital room and looks around.

She'd been pretending to be out of it all day. She had remained still as the nurses, doctors, and staff members tried to determine how her fingers got mutilated. To them the wounds looked self-inflicted. And all she thought about was finishing what Yvonna had started, whether she wanted to or not.

"About time she's gone," she says aloud to herself, referring to Penny. "I can't take one more day of 'Man Hands Penny' touchin' me."

Gabriella eases out of bed. Her clothes were so soaked with blood that they destroyed them immediately after tearing them off her body. On a mission she moves toward the door. When she doesn't see lurking hospital officials staring at her, she quickly dips back into the room and places a pair of hospital slippers on her bare feet.

"I gotta get outta here before these no-good–ass doctors try to drug me up again. That's all the fuck they know how to do. Drug a bitch up, and shit."

Once the slippers are on, she snatches the needles out of her arm. Her right hand throbs with pain, but before long she feels nothing. Crazy bastards are known for having a strong threshold for pain, and there is no one crazier than this bitch. Although the bandages do make it harder for her to move around, she walks hurriedly through the hallway. Dipping into each room, she manages to steal enough clothing to conceal her body. The only problem is, she looks worse than she ever has in her life.

"Yvonna, I sure hope you know what I'm doing for us. I'd never be caught dead in this bullshit *if* it wasn't for you."

Yvonna can't respond because Gabriella has totally taken over, and now all hell is about to break loose. Before leaving, she manages to steal a syringe. Wearing a run-down old brown cap, with the word "moose" stitched on the front, and an oversized black shirt and oversized jeans, she exits the hospital in a frenzy.

"Now where can I go?"

The sun is bright and cars whiz up and down the street. Everyone is in a rush, and so is she. With the money fund being spent entirely on fashion, she's broke. She needs a sucka to take her in. And then it dawns on her.

"I feel like seein' me some old-ass Penny today!" she declares.

There's No Stopping Her Now

Gabriella is in Chevy Chase, on the side of a building, looking for the perfect prey. It doesn't take her long to find one. With her plan embedded firmly in her mind, she decides to execute it. The pretty target, with almond-colored skin, that she spots is pretty and fly. She takes notice of the designer jeans she wears, along with her stylish red Prada jacket.

Gabriella walks hurriedly toward her, and the mark is carrying five or six shopping bags in her hands. When the girl deactivates her alarm, Gabriella sees the silver Range Rover and is proud of her choice.

I swear, I be knowin' how to pick 'em.

The license plates reads: CRYSTAL.

I hate bitches named Crystal, she thinks.

The woman is opening her trunk, when Gabriella yells, "So you still gonna fuck wit my man, huh?" She has her hands on her hips, and the girl's pretty green eyes widen, believing she must be talking to someone else.

"Are you talkin' to me?"

"Don't play games wit me. Keep that shit up and I'll stomp you every which way."

"I'm serious. I think you got the wrong person."

"Bitch, you know who I am! I'm sick of you sneakin' behind my back and sleepin' wit what's mine!" Gabriella points to herself.

"Are you kidding me?" the girl says as she accidentally drops her bags.

Gabriella notices a brown shoe box with white lettering and knows it can be none other than Christian Louboutin's signature atop it.

"James still messin' wit you?"

She can't believe how gullible the girl is. Not only is she buying the story, she is name-dropping.

"Yes, I'm talkin' about James's bitch ass." Gabriella steps closer. "My fuckin' husband, James! And since you don't know how to listen, I'ma have to make you!"

The girl looks like she is about to shit herself when Gabriella balls up her fist.

"Please don't hurt me. I'm sorry! I really am." She begins to cry. "I knew he was married, but he told me he didn't want to be with her because she had let herself go. Not saying that you let yourself go," she offers as an apology, looking at Gabriella's drab clothing. "He's supposed to be moving in with me next week, and everything. If I knew you were still in the picture, I wouldn't have ever continued to sleep with him."

"Well, that's not good enough, bitch. I'm 'bout to kick your ass so you will know better in the future."

Gabriella is preparing to hit her square in the face to set the tone, when she says, "What if we go approach him together? I'll tell him to his face it's over. Just please don't hit me. If I fight, my father won't let me be in his fashion show next month."

What the fuck? Gabriella thinks. "You just might've saved yourself from an ass whuppin'." She jumps inside the truck. "Let's go then. I gotta make a stop first."

Gabriella makes the unsuspecting girl run her all around town. It is nice being chauffeured. First they stop at Target, where she picks up a few items. And when Crystal tries to stay in the car, Gabriella forces her to get out. There is no way on earth she is letting her moneybags, car-driving ass get away. Besides, Crystal has credit cards and cash, and Gabriella realizes she suddenly hit the jackpot!

After getting all she needs, compliments of her hostage, they get back in the truck. Gabriella allows her to talk as she writes a letter, sealing the envelope. Now all she needs is a mailbox. While she looks around for one, she occasionally sizes up the girl. What Gabriella isn't sure of is the other woman's shoe size, so she decides to ask.

"What happened to your hand?" Crystal asks, turning left and right on the streets leading to James's barbershop in D.C.

"None of your business. Look, pull over up the street. I gotta fart and I don't wanna blow you away in here."

The girl looks at her and wrinkles up her face. "Did you just say 'fart'?"

"Yes, and you might be rich, but I know you know what the fuck a fart is. So, unless you want me to blow this muthafucka out, I suggest you pull over."

The girl pulls over. The moment she does, Gabriella says, "Cute shoes! What size are they?"

"Eight and a half." She smiles.

"Perfect." Gabriella lunges the butcher knife she just bought at Target into the girl's stomach. Crystal's eyes bulge and she turns a shade of red. She touches the knife's handle like it will go away, and Gabriella pushes it deeper and twists it into her abdomen.

"Don't fight it. Just let it go. It's over. You had a nice life, and I'm sure your family will give you a rock star funeral."

The girl looks at her and tears stream down her face. Why had she trusted a stranger? She looks back down at the knife and back at Gabriella again. And Gabriella, being the impatient bitch that she is, says, "Damn slut, would you die already! I got shit to do!"

So she pushes it deeper inside Crystal and pounds the end of the handle with her fist for added measure. And finally the girl falls back onto her plush cream-colored leather seat and closes her eyes.

"Thank you! I was so *not feeling* the drawn-out–ass death scene."

Gabriella jumps out of the car and runs to the driver's side and opens her door. The girl's body drops halfway out and she pulls her completely into the street. She is just about to leave, until she remembers the knife has her fingerprints on it; and Crystal is still wearing the shoes she wants.

But when she attempts to take the knife out, it doesn't move easily. So Gabriella places a foot, which is covered with a hospital slipper, on her victim's chest, balances herself, and—with her good hand—yanks it out.

"Got it!" she cheers, raising the knife in the air. It is dripping with blood.

Realizing there's nothing to cheer about, she puts her arm down and wipes the blood onto the girl's jacket. And then she takes the shoes off her feet and jumps back into the truck. A ten-year-old girl stands in shock, witnessing the entire scene.

"Oh, don't worry. She's just drunk. She'll be okay."

With that, she slams the car door shut and peels

into traffic. Being the multitasker that she is, she runs over and over in her mind what she plans to do, and to whom she plans to do it. She sees her plans so clear in her mind that she smiles with delight.

"I'll have my way in not much longer," she says aloud.

Once she gets far enough away from the scene, she rummages through the girl's shopping bags. She is disappointed when she realizes her taste isn't as grand as she had hoped.

"Damn! I didn't take you for a mediocre-type bitch." Gabriella sighs. "I woulda neva picked this brown dress with your skin tone." She shakes her head in outrage.

With her clothing choices limited, she wiggles into the best of the worst, settling upon the grim brown dress. The dress is not as comfortable as the hospital clothes, even though it is her size.

What the fuck did you do to our body, Yvonna? Eating out all the time, and shit! She decides to keep the dress on, despite the slight discomfort, and eases into the stolen pair of shoes.

"I'll give you credit for these," she says, looking at the pumps against her toned legs. "You most definitely know how to pick a fly pair of shoes." She throws the hospital gear out the window and searches for good theme music.

"Damn! Not the Carter Three," she says, excitedly moving in her seat. She loves Lil Wayne. "Who knew you fucked with Weezy?"

She places the CD in and allows his mellow voice to run through her body. Then she looks through the Target bag to be sure she has everything she needs to carry out her plans.

"Okay . . . let's see. One syringe, one bottle of liquid Drano, one comb, one brush, two paper bags." Then she digs into the girl's purse and pulls out some credit cards and cash. "Okay, a little bit of money and some plastic." She places the truck into drive. "I got everything I need. Now lets get down to business!"

The Start Of Somethin' Vengeful

"Yeah, this look likes the perfect place!"

It is late in the evening and the sky has turned to a purple hue. Gabriella places the stolen Range Rover in park and jumps out. She has been cruising around in the SUV like she owns the bitch. She stands out as she struts down the small block that she happened upon in Southeast D.C. Crackheads and dope fiends are plenty in this area, and they are exactly who she is looking for.

"Now which one of you funky bastards do I want?"

She scans the crowd for the thickest, nappiest, most bushy-headed muthafucka she can find. "Aha!" She smiles, quickly identifying her match. "Excuse me."

The crackhead, who is about six feet tall, dark-skinned and thin, fixes the old black dress coat he's wearing. He smooths out his crusted beard with his hands and says, "No, excuse me! And we can excuse each other for the whole night if you want to." He is strutting like he is straight out of an old Colt 45 commercial.

Gabriella laughs and says, "Honey, I wouldn't give you the time of day if I were driving eighty miles an hour and you were standing in front of my car."

"Well, *excuuussse* me." His breath stinks of infection and alcohol.

"Great, you a drunk too." She backs up and places her bandaged hand on her hip. "Look, *Pookie*, you wanna make some cash or what?"

"Hell yeah! What you want me to do to you?" He claps his rusty hands together and licks what's left of his dried-up lips.

"For starters you can stop thinkin' about this pussy 'cause it ain't gonna happen, 'Mr. Roach.' " He's offended, but he remains silent. "Now I want you to brush and comb that nest of a head of yours over this bag." She pulls out the comb and brush and hands it to him. "Then I want you to give it to me when you're done. Capeesh?"

"What kind of freaky shit is this?"

"None of your damn business." Gabriella tears the brown paper bag open and moves toward a small patch of grass. She places the bag on the ground and says, "Now get over here." The man follows, although slightly confused.

"You sure you not gonna tell me what's going on?"

Gabriella smacks him in the face so hard that for a second he's sober. He rubs his bruised face and looks like a child who got punished for disrespecting his mother.

"So, are you gonna stop actin' like Sherlock Holmes, or are you gonna be the crackhead I'm paying you for?" The man sees something crazed in her eyes and gets on his knees.

"I knew you had some sense in that fucked-up body of yours."

As requested, he bends over so that his head is directly above the ripped bag. He combs and brushes his hair over the top of it. His eyes meet hers in between the strokes, and the fear-stricken man is afraid she'll hit him again. Dandruff, tiny hair follicles, and even small bugs fall on top of the bag.

"That's so yuck-a-licious!" she proclaims.

"Is that enough?"

She examines the mess. "Comb that knot a few more times," she orders. He does. "Good. Now fold it up in a ball and put it in here." After he folds the bag closed, keeping its contents in tact, she holds another bag open and he drops it inside. Then she folds that bag several times shut.

"Here is your comb and brush," he says, handing it to her.

She frowns at the filthy articles. "Honey, you couldn't pay me to take that shit back. Keep it. You need it more than me."

Gabriella rummages through the Target bag

she's holding and says, "Now let me pay you." She pulls out a few items, including the bloodstained butcher knife, and says, "Oh . . . can you hold this for me for a second? It's in the way and I'm looking for your money."

"What the fuck?" He grabs the knife by the handle, looking at it from side to side. "What were you cooking?"

"Nothing," she says, accepting the weapon back with a napkin to avoid getting new fingerprints on it after just recently wiping *hers* off. She places it carefully in the bag. "I'm so silly. Your money is right here in my pocket. Take this one-hundred-dollar bill. I'm paying you for your silence and your trifling ways. But you betta neva—*eva*—tell anybody you saw me. Understand?" She points at him. He nods in agreement. "Great! Get your high on. I'm outta here. Oh yeah, do you know where I can buy a gun?"

Reluctantly he directs her down the street and she leaves the lowly man exactly where she had met him. She adjusts the rearview mirror so that she can see herself in it and says, "I love when shit comes together!"

Old Bitches, Old Tricks

Gabriella parks the stolen Range Rover a few blocks down and walks to Penny's house with her Target bag in hand. She doesn't knock right away. She is trying to get herself in mode to be meek and humble, like Yvonna, and is finding it very difficult to pull off. Taking a deep breath, she says, "I'm just gonna have to do the best I can."

She knocks twice and looks like a sad puppy.

"Yvonna? What are you doin' here?" She doesn't seem that happy to see her.

"You not happy to see me?" she asks softly.

"Oh . . . yeah." She stares at her body as if something's wrong and then focuses on her eyes. They look different to Penny. "Of course, I am. But you're s'posed to be in the hospital."

"Yeah, well, I hate hospitals. Can I come in or not?"

"Of course, chile." She opens the door wider and Gabriella strolls inside.

When the door closes, she sees Bradshaw sitting on the sofa. She squints her eyes and wonders how long it will take her to rip his throat out, until she remembers that she just might need his ass.

"Bradshaw? What you doing here?"

He stands and walks up to her, looking at her hand.

"He was worried 'bout ya. And decided to stop on by to check on ya. He says he hadn't heard from ya in a while. I told him you hurt yourself and was in the hospital."

"I guess."

"I didn't know you had a boyfriend."

"I didn't know I had one either." Gabriella examines his fashionable long-sleeved white dress shirt, pink cashmere vest, and blue jeans.

"How did you get my address?"

"I drop you off all the time. What are you talking about?"

Gabriella doesn't answer.

"Anyway, you always told me that if I hadn't heard from you in a couple of days, I should come looking for you. So I'm here."

That damn Yvonna! "Oh yeah, I remember." She is lying.

He places his hands on her shoulders. She despises the way he made Yvonna lose reason, and she is determined not to be easily seduced. She is in control, not him.

Gabriella snatches herself away and says, "Well, I'm fine. You can leave now."

"Can I talk to you before I leave? Alone?" he asks. They both look at Penny. "It's kind of private."

"Oh . . . I'm sorry. I have a prayer circle that'll be startin' in 'bout fifteen minutes. But ya welcome to take him downstairs, though. I cleaned up for you." She walks up to Gabriella and looks into her eyes again, but Gabriella looks away. "How's your hand?"

"Doesn't hurt one bit." Gabriella focuses on the multicolored housecoat.

"That's good. Real good. I'm glad you're home." Penny continues looking at her. "Oh, and some movie company folks stopped by, wantin' my input on your story. I chased 'em out of here. They wanted to offer me a lot of money, and I just wanted you to know."

"Doesn't matter. Well, I guess we'll go downstairs now."

Right before she opens the door to the basement, Penny says, "And, Yvonna, does the box need to be dropped off today?"

"What box?"

"The box you told me to keep."

Not knowing what she means, Gabriella says, "Oh. That box. No, it's fine."

She has no idea what the old fool is saying, but she decides to give it no more attention than she already has. Penny, on the other hand, watches her until she is completely out of sight.

"So what was so important?" she asks him as they sit on the foot of the bed.

"I wanted to check on you. But what's up wit your hand?"

"A long story."

"A'ight. At first, I thought you were fucked up with me for being distant when we were together. I got a lot on my mind, and you know I'm tryin' to get some extra cash to get my daughter. They tellin' me if I can't afford twenty-four-hour in-home care that they may never let her stay with me. She's in the foster care system now."

"Look, I'm not tryin' to be rude, but I don't care."

His face tightens up and he takes a deep breath.

"It doesn't matter. It's not that deep," Gabriella remarks.

"What does that mean?"

"What does it sound like?" she says as she stands up to get undressed. When she's naked, she turns around and looks at him. "You wanna fuck, or what?"

It isn't what he had planned, but they spend the next thirty minutes having passionate sex. There is something about the way her body moves that he likes.

"You were different tonight. And did I tell you how I love the weight you gained?" He adjusts the covers and his pants, which are hanging over the end of the bed.

"I don't remember, but I move different 'cause you used to fuckin' Yvonna's cornball ass, not me."

" 'Yvonna'?" he asks, separating his body from hers to look into her eyes. "You saying that you *not* Yvonna?"

"What you think? Yvonna ain't got shit on my fuck game."

Bradshaw sits up in the bed and leans against the headboard. "Then tell me 'bout you."

"Oh, you not scared?"

"Scared of what?"

"Of all the things people say I did. And all the people they say I hurt."

"Naw. I'm interested. I wanna know what makes you tick. You're different."

"We are. And, personally, I don't think there's anything wrong with us."

"Us?"

"Yeah, me and Yvonna. I think people just need to let us be. We might not be like everyone thinks we should be, but we're real. I'm real. And we don't need no medicine to change us."

"Are you her protector?"

"Something like that. I think I'm more into protecting me than anything. If I don't, Yvonna's gullible ass would kill us both. She'll let them doctors tell her all kinds of shit. And before we know it, we'll be crazy."

Bradshaw can't believe his ears, and Gabriella loves the attention she is getting from him. So many times the doctors and professionals spent trying to get rid of her. It felt good being accepted.

"I like you. And I hope you stay around."

"It doesn't bother you that I've hurt so many people?"

"I like you just the way you are."

Gabriella smiles, until she notices something in his eyes isn't right.

"Are you playing games wit me? Are you fuckin' wit me?" She shoots daggers at him with her eyes. " 'Cause it's not a good idea to fuck wit me."

"I'm not . . . fuckin' wit you." If he hadn't been scared before, he is now. "I'm bein' honest."

There is a long pause of silence between them. He reaches for his pants, which have been on the bed the entire time they made love, and pulls out another condom.

"You ready to go another round?"

She smiles and says, "You just try and keep up."

Zoned Out

Swoopes is in the cafeteria eating for the first time in three days. He hasn't been out of his room since he has been raped. And he doesn't know who the fuck has assaulted him. When he looks around, anybody within a few feet of him could've been a suspect. He imagines them talking behind his back; and, most important, he reasons that unless he finds out soon who took his respect, that offender would most certainly try to get some boy ass again.

"Damn, where you been at, homie?" Tree asks, walking up behind him.

On edge, and not recognizing his voice yet, Swoopes reaches under the table, lifts his pants, and touches the homemade shank taped to his leg. But when he realizes who it is, he lets it fall back down to position.

"You been missin' in action."

"Yeah, I wasn't feelin' good," Swoopes says, faking a cough.

"That shit ain't contagious, is it?" Tree jokes.

"I can't call it." Swoopes laughs.

"I'm just fuckin' wit you, youngblood. Everything cool?"

Swoopes moves his food around his plate. "Yeah, I'm good. What's up wit you, though?"

"Ain't shit. You know they shipped Corn's ass to another prison last night."

Swoopes looks up from his plate and at Tree, to be sure he heard him correctly.

"They shipped him to another prison? For what?"

"I don't know. Somebody said he turned feds, and they had to get him outta here for protection. I couldn't stand that nigga no way."

Swoopes doesn't have an appetite; but after hearing about Corn's transfer, he isn't sure he'll ever be able to eat again.

"You a'ight, Swoo?"

Swoopes moves around on the hard plastic chair, trying to get comfortable. It isn't working. He swallows hard and opens another button on his shirt so that the heat rising from his skin can escape. "Oh . . . uh . . . yeah. I'm fine."

"You don't look like it. You look like you about to pass out, and shit."

He never—*ever*—considered Corn. He didn't peg him for the raping type. And now that his name is mentioned, he wonders why he hadn't. Even though rape is a foul-ass way to get a nigga back, if it was his method, it certainly worked.

"Look, man. I'm 'bout to roll. You want the rest of my food?"

"Hell yeah," Tree says, reaching for his bread.

When Tree extends his hand and reaches for Swoopes's meal, he recognizes the large knuckles and how rough they look. He hasn't expected to remember exact details about that day, because he wants to forget it. But there is no denying that after noticing Tree's hands, he is sure Tree is the one who has violated him.

"Hey, you still comin' by my cell tonight, right?" Tree tears off the bread he got from Swoopes's plate. "Na-na-now, I got some smoke and drink in my room."

Swoopes's body feels light, and his knees buckle. He's heard that speech defect before, when he was younger. And just like the memory of Tree's hands were recalled to mind, so was his impediment. It was both unique and stupid, so how could Swoopes not remember?

Now there are men who are considered tough, rough, and strong. But there is no man, in the *entire* prison, who possesses the strength that Swoopes has in that moment. It takes everything in his power not to rip him apart right where he sits. But he is smart. He has to be. If he wants him—like he wants him—he has no choice but to fall back and wait. Swoopes inhales and keeps his chest filled with the oxygen he needs to handle the situation.

"If you got smoke and drink, you know I'm there." Swoopes smirks.

"I'm serious, Swoo." He continues eating the bread. The fucking pet name of "Swoo" pisses Swoopes off.

"Swoopes, man. My name is Swoopes."

"What?" Tree laughs, looking up at him.

"I ain't tryin' to be funny, but my name is Swoopes. Not Swoo." It is bad enough that Tree took his ass, and even worse that he has to wait to knock his block off. But he has no intention of letting this bitch-ass nigga continue to call him by a personal pet name he'd created.

"Oh . . . no doubt. I meant Swoopes." Tree senses something is wrong, but he doesn't think things through. "I gotta rap to you 'bout somethin' later too."

"Don't worry. I'll be there. You can count on that."

Tree's eyes can barely open because bandages appear to be covering his lids. And from what he can see through the cracks, he isn't in his room. Not to mention that the mattress is much softer than the one in his cell. And when he tries to move, pain shoots through every limb in his body.

"Don't move," a woman's voice advises. "You are not the same man as you were yesterday."

Not the same man I was yesterday? Fuck does she mean? he thinks.

"Wha-what's goin' on?"

"You've been badly hurt. We found you in your cell on the floor in a puddle of your own blood and liquor."

A flash of Swoopes coming into his room and drinking liquor is the last thing he could remember. He recalls himself preparing to finish Yvonna's request, and he ended up getting dealt with. Everything else is a blur. He had placed himself in a cage with a lion and was torn to pieces.

"So what's wrong wit me?"

"It appears you got intoxicated and got into a fight. You know it's a violation to have liquor in prison, Mr. Green."

"I ain't tryin' to hear that shit right now! I need details on my condition!"

"Well, you betta be trying to hear it, because your life has changed forever." Her voice loses all concern and is replaced with contempt. "Do you know who did this?"

"No! I—I don't," he lies.

"Are you sure?"

"Yes, I am! Now tell me what the fuck is up."

"Your spine is fractured. The skin over your eyes is almost completely gone. You have severe cuts on your face, and . . . and . . ." The woman hesitates and doesn't continue her list of injuries.

"What? What is it?"

"And your penis has been completely severed from your body. We couldn't find it, so it could not be reattached."

"Awwwwwwwwwwwwwwwwwwwwwwwwwww!" Tree screams.

"Let me get the counselor."

Three weeks later

The prison is on lockdown after the attack on Tree; and as usual, no one knows shit. And because Swoopes is considered a *friend,* no one suspects him.

Swoopes made a decision earlier in the morning to kill members of Tree's family when he is free in fourteen months, but he needs addresses first. He could hand this duty to members of the YBM, but he does not want them knowing he was fucked. It isn't enough that he forced Tree into an alcoholic stupor, before beating him over and over, finally cutting his penis off with his shank and flushing it down the toilet. He needs and wants more to be done.

The only reason Swoopes left him alive is because he knows that it is next to impossible for a man to go about the world without a dick. Anyway, he feels people give *death* too much credit as a form of punishment. And since Swoopes has never died, he can't vouch that it would be good enough for Tree. For all Swoopes knows, death could bring a reward that Tree's slum ass doesn't deserve. *But . . .* he could vouch that life, if fucked up enough, could be a living hell.

While rummaging through Tree's personal mail, he happens upon a stack of letters. Most of them came from a PO address, and for a moment he's discouraged. *I need a fuckin' address. Where does your family live, muthafucka?*

As he skims through the letters, he notices a girl's name on an envelope: Treyana. *What you got to do with this shit?* He knows her from his hometown, and he is trying to add things up. He opens a few of the letters and reads briefly through them. But when he sees one of the pictures, he stumbles. *Yvonna? What the fuck!* He doesn't understand why the letters are from Treyana, but the pictures are of Yvonna. Wanting time to quarterback the whole situation, he takes the letters and walks to his cell.

He's grateful he still doesn't have a celly because he needs extreme privacy. As he lies down, he reads them all, one by one. *None of these make any sense!*

Jo Cramer enters into the room, right before he answers his own question.

"Is it a good time now?" he asks, referring to Swoopes's magazines.

"Yo! Fuck is you so pressed for?!" Swoopes yells, tucking the letters behind him.

Jo is so startled that he temporarily forgets what

he came for. "I—I just wanted something to read the . . . Uh . . . you told me I could . . . read the magazines. So I came by to . . . uh . . . see . . . if I could get them now."

"You know what!" Swoopes leaps off his bunk, opens his locker, and grabs the magazines. Next he slams him so hard in the face with them that Jo's bottom lip cracks open and bleeds. "Now get the fuck outta here before I break ya jaw!"

Jo runs down the hall with the magazines. *Thirsty-ass nigga.* Now alone, Swoopes holds the letter that originally caught his attention. He sits down on his bunk and his feet remain planted on the floor. His muscles buckle involuntarily, due to how angry he is.

Opening the letter once more, he reads the poem; and again it makes no sense.

"Fuck does this mean, you crazy bitch?"

This time he pushes his anger aside and focuses on the words, not necessarily their meaning:

> *You are I.*
> *And you are what I want.*
> *I am her who can't live without him.*
> *You are my heart beat.*
> *I'd rather be raped*
> *And*
> *I'd rather be tortured*
> *Until I say when.*
> *Because it's*
> *Not going to do me any good at all*

To be without you. I said
That until it's all said and
Done
That you are what I
Want.
You . . . not him.
When you left, I felt killed.

He stands up and holds the paper so tightly in his hand that it crumbles. She used the same code they used when he was a member of the YBM.

"Bilal must've taught her," he says aloud, shaking his head.

He reads it out loud now, the way it should be read: " 'I want him beat, raped, and tortured. When it's all said and done, I want him killed.' "

He balls the letter up and looks out before him. Now shit just got serious. Did she know about his involvement in her case? *Naw. It's impossible.* He tears down the pictures he has of sexy women on his wall. Even the pictures of his celly's children get taken down. He replaces them all with one picture of Yvonna.

From the moment Bilal introduced him to her, he didn't like her. He didn't even know why, and he had no memory of them meeting as children. But he did know that he hated the air she breathed.

He decides to chill out in prison. He'll play by the rules and play their little games—something he never considered before. If he felt himself slipping, he would refocus on his goal by looking at her face in the picture. He doesn't want anything to interfere with his release. She'll be the first person he'll see when his feet hit the pavement.

Swoopes smiles. For the first time in life, he has inspiration, and her name is Yvonna Harris.

"I hope you ready for me, bitch."

Everything Comes
to the Light

"I can't tell you no more than I already have." Avante sits on the couch with his pants unbuttoned and his shirt half open.

"Maybe there's something or somebody you left out," Jensen says. "Think."

Avante looks up at the officers with disgust. And again the lights flicker on and off, like they had earlier. They ignore it.

"There has to be something else," Jensen persists. "One detail overlooked."

He stands up and his clothes fail to cover his body securely, exposing his white cotton boxers a little around the waist. "You're starting to make me think I'm a suspect."

"Not yet, but you act like it. And why didn't you tell the FBI?" Samuels asks.

He looks at them. "Because I wasn't looking for special consideration."

" 'Special consideration'? To find your wife?" The lights flicker again, but this time they take a little longer to come back on. "Do you need to change your bulbs, or something?" Officer Jensen inquires as he looks up again—the large hairs in his beefy nose are showing.

Intoxicated, Avante says, "Maybe it's her ghost, or somethin'." He laughs in bad taste.

"That's not funny, Mr. Plier."

"It is to me. And, anyway, it can't be a single-bulb problem, because all the lights in the house go out," he says with an attitude.

"You need to relax." Jensen is sick of his mouth.

"That's easier said than done."

When the lights flicker off this time, they are unable to continue with their conversation because they are in complete darkness.

"Where is your electric box?" Officer Samuels asks. "Something must be wrong."

"It's outside"—Avante swallows his liquor—"in the back of the house."

They all walk into the darkness of the night and around back.

"Got a flashlight?" Jensen asks, stepping up to the extra-large panel.

In a drunken stupor Avante pats his pockets. "Naw, not on me."

The cops shake their heads, tiring of him quickly.

"Well, do you have a key to open the box at least?" Samuels asks, using the light on his phone to see a little. "Wait! It's open. But hold up! What the fuck is that smell?"

He moves away from it. Because truth be told, there is only one smell on earth that is fouler than any smell imaginable.

"I don't know, but I'm about to find out." Jensen pulls the handle.

Avante stops and turns around, just in time to see Treyana's head roll out, followed by other parts of her body. The blood has soaked into the panel, causing the circuits to trip and the lights to flicker. She's been in there since the day after she was murdered.

"Oh, my Godddddd!" Avante cries, seeing his wife's dismembered body. *"Plllease help meeeeee!"*

He rushes toward the scene and the officers stop him. After all, she's not his wife anymore. She is now homicide evidence.

All Closed Eyes
Don't Sleep

Penny is snoring for points until, in between a heavy breath, she feels pressure against her body. She opens her eyes and is horrified to see Yvonna lying directly on top of her, with her head resting upon her breasts as if she were a child.

"What are you doin'?" Penny is scared to make a sudden move.

"Listening."

"To what?"

"Your breaths. You're a hard sleeper. I've been here for almost ten minutes," she says, looking up at her before resting her head comfortably. "You really shouldn't sleep that hard. Someone could take full advantage of you . . . if they wanted."

"What are ya doin' in my room, chile?"

Coldly she says, "I wanted to see how fast a heart beats, before it stops."

"You betta be tellin' me somethin', 'cause I don't understand what you sayin'."

"Cut the bullshit. You know exactly what I'm sayin'."

"I don't know!"

Gabriella places a gun barrel to Penny's head, all while maintaining her position on Penny's body. *Click.* She cocks the hammer.

"Do you understand now?"

"Gabriella?"

"In the flesh."

"Why are you doin' this?"

"Because you a meddlin' bitch who won't go away."

"Don't do this. I care about ya."

"You don't care about anybody but yourself."

"I *do* love ya. And I'm askin' you to spare my life."

"It's too late." Gabriella laughs. She is about to pull the trigger, when Penny jerks her body roughly and the gun falls out of Gabriella's hand and onto the floor. Gabriella tries to reach for it, until she feels cold steel against the side of her waist.

"Get up, bitch, before I blow your ass to the future!" Penny turns on the lamp.

"I'm not—" Gabriella is cut off, due to Penny firing into the wall, before placing the gun back on Gabriella's waist.

Boom! "The next one's goin' in your body. Now get the fuck up!"

Gabriella eases off Penny. When she does, Penny

stands up and looks into her eyes. She maintains her aim at Gabriella, who backs against the wall. Gabriella feels a little lightheaded, and her stomach feels queasy the moment she stands, and she wonders why. Penny squints her eyes to look at her. Something is different about her; but in the dark of the night, it's too hard to tell.

"I'm smarter than you thought, huh?"

Gabriella thinks she talks like a runaway slave, so how could Penny possibly be intelligent?

"Yvonna gave me a code phrase. She said if I ever doubted it was her, I should ask, 'Does the box need to be dropped off today?' "

Recalling the question from a few days ago, Gabriella says, "That's what that dumb shit was about?"

"If that's what you choose to calls it. Alls I know is if you were my Yvonna, ya woulda said, 'I already mailed it.' But you didn't know the ansa."

Gabriella doesn't want to admit it, but Yvonna played it smart.

"If you thought I *wasn't* Yvonna, why would you let me in your house?"

"Because you use ta go away afta some time. But . . . I see she's gettin' worse. I talked to Terrell Shines and Jona, though. They told me what I gotta do to help, but ya gets the best treatment if you recommit yaself. Jona says she tried, but you won't consent. They gonna keep you safe and cure ya, but you gots to let 'em."

It pisses Gabriella the fuck off that Terrell and

Jona can't stay the fuck out of her business, and she can't wait to get at them.

"And just what the fuck did they tell you to do to 'help' me?" she asks, making the universal quotation signs with her fingers.

"I already started. I been puttin' medicine in the food."

Gabriella laughs. "I already know about the tea." Penny is surprised and wonders how she knows. "And I don't eat anything else here."

"You ate *packaged* foods."

Gabriella figures that's what caused the queasiness. "You's a dumb bitch."

"I'm doin' it 'cause I love you. And placing the medicine in the bottled water was one of the only ways I knew how."

The water? she thinks. *I ain't been drinking the water.* "You're a liar!"

"I don't lie, 'specially 'bout peoples I care about. Anyway, you gonna get on out my house right now, and I'ma be prayin' for you from afar, till I think of somethin' else. And the cops been callin' me. I ain't met with 'em yet, but I gots plans to meet wit 'em tomorrow."

Gabriella clenches her fist and takes one step toward Penny, thinking she could take her.

"Do you really want to test my aim?"

"Them fuckin' pig cops gonna get what they deserve too."

Gabriella is getting angrier; and even though Penny has the gun, she is slightly frightened.

"Get out of my house!" She stiffens her arms and refreshes her aim. "Now, I loves Yvonna, but I loves myself mo and won't hesitate to put one in ya and pray to the good Lord above lada." Gabriella's eyes narrow.

"Okay, I'm leavin'," Gabriella responds, smirking.

"Now that I *already* know fa'sho! So we gonna do it like this. You gonna back up all the way out of my house. If you don't make no sudden moves, you'll live. Are we clear, chile?"

Penny lifts Gabriella's weapon off the floor and tucks it in the back of her cotton black pajama pants. She's like a thug off a D.C. corner. For a woman of God, she sure handles her weapons like a pro.

"I need to get a few things downstairs. Can I?"

"Out!"

"Well, can I have my gun?"

"Get out of here now!" Penny yells, cutting her off.

Gabriella backs all the way out of Penny's house like she was told. When she is completely gone, Penny makes a call. Yvonna would not be safe in her condition, and Penny wants her to have help.

"Nine-one-one. How may I help you?"

"Yes, I need the police. Please send them right away."

When Crazies Attack

Gabriella looks through the window of Jona's house. She's contemplating on how to get inside so she can kill her. She has had her address for a while and only planned to use it if she threatened to take her freedom again. When Jona spoke to Penny, Gabriella felt she did just that.

Jona works busily on her computer; Gabriella wonders if whatever held her attention had something to do with her. She holds in her hands the names of the additional people she plans to exact revenge on. She didn't include the names of the people Yvonna hated, because she already has their names etched firmly in her mind and on her body.

This is Gabriella's personal list; and because of it, it is the most dangerous of all. Staring at the list, her hands shake with rage:

HATE LIST 2: LOOSE CANNON

Jona
Terrell
Samuels
Jensen
Lily

She is still staring at the list when a Rottweiler, whose head is so large it bends the corner of the small brick house before the rest of his body, runs toward her. She mistakenly drops the list on the ground and runs for her life.

Jona looks up from her computer when she hears her dog barking. She walks toward the window. She sees no one. Wanting to know what caused Titan to bark, she decides to go outside. Before leaving, she grabs her loaded twelve-gauge shotgun, which stays by the door. She opens the door and walks carefully outside.

"Titan!" she calls. He runs to her.

"What happened?" she asks, although she knows he can't answer.

The dog's heavy panting plays in the background. Squinting her eyes, she sees someone staring at her up the street, but she can't see his or her face. She looks at her dog and then back up the street, but the person is gone. Patting Titan on top of his massive cranium, she says, "Good boy. Good boy."

Whoever it was, Titan clearly ran them away. While the dog licks her hand, she looks down on her green lawn and notices a white piece of paper. She bends down and picks it up; her dog is still beside her. Opening it fully, she sees a typed sheet of paper with a group of names, including hers. Losing her balance, she stumbles against her house and rests against it for support.

"It was Yvonna," she says to the dog and the night air. "Oh, my Gawd, it was Yvonna!"

The Station

The forensic department is spotless as clerks move about, trying to provide the evidence necessary to solve cases. Officers Jensen and Samuels stand in front of Cheryl Hanks, a beautiful white clerk with blond hair.

"So how soon can we get the prints from the electrical panel? And the Bernice Santana case?" Samuels asks as Cheryl sits in front of her computer, scanning through millions of fingerprints.

"I'm going to work on it as quickly as possible, but I can't make any promises or provide you with a firm date. You know we're backed up around here."

"But this is the Yvonna Harris case," Jensen chimes in. "And we need this back ASAP."

"I know what and who it's about, Jensen."

"Well, what's the problem?" Jensen persists.

She sighs. "Nothing."

"Well, make this one special," Jensen says, placing his hand on her back.

"I'll do what I can."

"Thanks, love."

When they walk away, Samuels asks, "You fuckin' her, ain't you?"

"What do you think?"

They laugh on the way to their next destination.

"What do you guys want with me?" Lily asks, sitting on the only available space on her couch. Her place is as trashy as ever.

"Lily, what are you doing to yourself?" Samuels looks around. Coming from "Sir Funks-a-lot," that carried a lot of weight. Literally.

"Yeah, Lily. This has gotten out of control." Jensen walks to her window and opens it. Cool, fresh air rushes inside.

"It smells like pussy that ain't been washed in twenty days in here," Samuels adds.

"You've had pussy that ain't been washed in twenty days?" Jensen asks.

"You haven't?"

They laugh and focus their attention back on Lily.

"I just want to be left alone."

"You know, if you want to kill yourself, there's a better way." Jensen knocks a bunch of trash out of a recliner to sit down. "You don't have to take the long route."

"Yeah. 'Cause ever since your partner died, you've been going downhill," Samuels opines.

"I don't want to talk about it."

"Well, you need to do somethin', and you need to do it soon," says Samuels, "because we need your help." He sits down on the other end of the sofa.

"I'm not interested in following Yvonna, if that's what you want. I want no part of that shit. I gave my entire life to the police department, and it hasn't been worth it."

"Damn it, Lily! Stop feelin' sorry for yourself and tell me what the fuck is going on!" Samuels's boisterous voice booms.

Instead of being angry, Lily drops her head and sobs. She's an emotional mess.

"I didn't know. . . . I swear I didn't know! But when I found out, I was afraid!"

"You didn't know what?" Samuels pries. "And what were you afraid of?"

"I didn't know Shonda did what she did." Lily continues crying heavily. "And when I found out, I never told anyone."

"Start from the beginning, Lily. Just start from the beginning."

The Day "Crazy Dave" Caught Up to Yvonna at the Hotel

"*Yvonna! Yvonna!*" *a male voice yelled from an undetermined location.*

When she didn't look, due to examining the car, the person became persistent. Turning toward the voice, she saw Swoopes in the passenger seat of a White Yukon Denali. He had a black eye patch over his left eye. She hadn't planned on seeing him and was quite aware of how he felt about her. She almost dropped her shopping bags due to being so frightened.

What the fuck is going on around here? *she thought. When Dave got out of the driver's seat and walked up on her, she was a little relieved they came together. She thought Swoopes was there to kill her.*

"I got to talk to you!" *he said frantically.*

"For what? And how you know I was here?"

"Sabrina told me—you weren't staying with her no more," he advised as a look of urgency came over his face. *"So I asked Cream and she told me where to find you."*

"Well, I can't talk now," she responded as she briefly looked him up and down. He looked so much like the rapper Young Buck, without the cornrows, that it was scary.

She turned to walk away, but he grabbed her wrist. He let her go, remembering the last time he held her against her will.

"Look," he said, glancing around to be sure no one was listening, *"the police been round the way askin' questions 'bout you. Somebody said you were in town."*

"What they want from me?" she questioned, looking over at Swoopes, who was frowning.

"Dave, come on man!" Swoopes hollered. *"We gotta be at the shop by seven! Ain't nobody got time for that bitch!"*

"Fuck you!" Yvonna yelled.

"Nigga, hold up," he said, turning around, irritated at his outburst. *"Look"*—he turned back to Yvonna— *"call me here."* He handed her a card that read: DAVE WALTERS, EACH ONE TEACH ONE. CHILDREN'S ADVOCATE.

"Whatever," she responded, taking the card from him and tossing it into one of her bags. *"I'll call you when I can. And what happened to his eye?"*

"It's a long story." With that, he dipped off. Her eyes

met Swoopes's once more before they sped off. He hated her and she felt it.

Later on that day Swoopes met up with Shonda in a run-down arcade center in Southeast D.C.

"Shonda, what you gonna do? You wastin' time when I need this bitch dead."

"I gotta be honest. I'm not feelin' the murder thing. I'm a cop, Swoopes."

"Well, you betta start feelin' it, cop!" he says, getting in her face.

"Why do you hate her so much?"

"I got my reasons."

His mind was made up and she knew it. "What if I set her up, instead?"

"Set her up how?"

"I'll frame her for a murder or somethin'."

"How the fuck you gonna do that?"

"I don't know. But I do know this girl from the Southwest who's a sharpshooter. And, on a camera, she'll look just like Yvonna—just as long as she doesn't show her entire face. We'll tail Yvonna. And when it's the right time, we'll make a move. I'll press the issue to everybody in my department that Yvonna's involved somehow. Before you know it, she'll be a suspected murderer."

"She's one now."

"And that's why it'll work."

Silence.

"This shit betta work!"

"It will. But look . . . when it's done, how much longer will you blackmail me?"

"Come on, Shonda! We go way back. You one of my favorite customers. I'll stop when I get what I want." He laughed. *"You can trust me."*

"What about the tape of me smokin' and buyin' from you? You gonna get rid of that too?"

"Not before I see this bitch locked up for whatever scheme you got hatched." Swoopes walked off and left her alone.

The next day she and hit woman Katrina Carber followed Yvonna all day. And when they saw her in the T. G. I. Friday's restaurant, they found the perfect person and the perfect situation to carry out Shonda's plan.

At T. G. I. Friday's restaurant

She placed both plates on Yvonna's side of the table.

"Bitch, I had enough of your shit!" Gabriella responded. *"One of them plates belong to me."*

The waitress rolled her eyes at Yvonna and walked off.

"She must've heard you cuss her out earlier," Yvonna replied. *"Don't even trip!"*

"I got somethin' for that bitch later," she responded as the waitress walked off.

"You heard that?" Shonda asked Katrina. They were seated at a nearby table and saw the interaction between Yvonna and the waitress.

"Yeah."

"But why is she talking to herself?" Katrina asked. "That bitch is crazy."

"I know. But fuck all that, I need you to pull this off. Now I paid you twenty-five hundred, and you'll get five thousand when you're finished."

"Where did you get that kind of money from?"

"Don't worry about it." She was not about to tell her that she stole the money from evidence at the precinct. And if she did, she feared she'd want more. "Meet the waitress when she get's off of work. Just don't forget to dress like her as much as possible. You already wear a similar hairstyle, but don't let the camera see your face. Side profiles are okay, because we need those shots. You got it?"

"How do I know you won't frame me for it?"

"Katrina, I got enough evidence on you to put you away for the rest of your life. I still have the weapon you used when you accidentally shot that pastor when he came out of the church 'cause you was trying to get somebody else. Trust me, if I wanted you behind bars, I could have you."

"Not if I kill you, instead," the hit woman said, raising her head and looking the cop square in the eyes.

Silence.

"You could kill me, but I gave your name to my people. *If you don't carry this shit through, they'll kill you, instead. We're in this together now. You may know who I am, but you haven't the slightest idea who they are."*

Katrina released the air from her chest and said, *"Why you doin' this, anyway? Ain't you the law?"*

"I don't know what I am anymore. But if you fuck this up, you won't be alive long enough to find out."

The night of the verdict

Shonda stood outside on the court steps. The day was beautiful; yet everything going on around her world felt gray. Katrina had done, as she was paid to do, and Jasmine McDonald had been murdered. Still, unless Yvonna was found guilty and sentenced to jail, Swoopes wouldn't find her work satisfactory. She pressed the button to accept the call from the prison. Her hand shook as she held the cell phone to her ear.

"Swoopes?"

"Who else, bitch?"

"Everything looks good. We don't think she'll get away with this."

"Well, I hope for your sake it sticks! 'Cause if it don't, your boys in blue gonna get that tape. My own brother set me up, and I shouldn't even be in here. Choosin' females before family. I want that nigga's world rocked."

"I've done all I can. Please don't ruin my career." She knew it didn't look promising that Yvonna would get locked up, even though she had told him otherwise. Her *doctors had managed to provide the jury with enough evidence to deem her crazy.*

"It betta stick," he said before hanging up.

"Who was that?" Lily asked, walking up behind her.

Shonda turned around and faced her. "Oh . . . uh, it was no one." She placed the phone into her pocket.

"But what could be taken from you, Shonda? Are you gonna talk to me? I'm your partner."

"I said nothing! Now leave me alone!"

Lily and Shonda ran up the steps leading to the court building. Once inside, they both took their seats in the jam-packed courtroom. Had it not been for other officers saving them seats, they would not have had one. They got there right before the jury gave their verdict.

"Jury, have you reached a verdict?" Judge Tyland asked.

Yvonna looked worried, and innocent, as she awaited their decision.

"Yes, we the people find Yvonna Harris not guilty by reason of insanity," an older black woman said. The courtroom erupted in noise.

Yvonna hugged her attorney and smiled at Dave, who had been supporting her the entire time.

"Order in the court!" Judge Tyland yelled.

The jury was so taken aback by what they saw on the hypnotism tapes, they felt she didn't deserve jail and needed help. The way she spoke of the rape when she was a child, and how her mother didn't believe her, tugged at their hearts.

Shonda dropped her head in defeat. She knew every-

thing she ever loved—and everybody she ever cared about—was about to be taken away. To make matters worse, killing Yvonna was no longer an option because she was in custody. Shonda sobbed heavily. From that point on she considered her life over.

Back at Lily's Apartment . . . The Tale Continues

Officer Jensen and Officer Samuels are in a trance. They can't believe their ears.

"Let me get this straight. Yvonna Harris did not commit the T. G. I. Friday's restaurant murder?" Officer Samuels asks.

With a drink in her hand, Lily shakes her head no.

"But she never fought the murder in court. I think she took the blame for it."

Lily laughs at both of them. "You two are so damn special! This is why this bitch won't rest until she ruins us. You're too busy thinking in terms of her being sane! Of course, she believed she did it! She believes she sees people and talks to them in public. She doesn't know who the fuck she murdered! Wake up!"

"Where are you goin' with this?" Jensen asks, insulted by her comment.

"*Think!* It's called 'autosuggestion.' She thought she did it, because she'd killed so many people. She could no longer tell the difference. Hell"—she gets up and pours herself another drink—"how many times have we used it to get suspects to confess? In the end she really thought she had murdered Jasmine McDonald."

The men look at each other and Jensen says, "Hey, can you pour us two drinks, please?"

She laughs and rinses off two dirty cups. "Sorry, I don't have any clean glasses."

"The dirtier, the better." Jensen rubs his forehead to reduce his headache.

"So what happened to Shonda? What made her kill herself?"

She hands them their drinks and sits down. "I was hoping you'd forget to ask me about that."

The day of Shonda's death

Lily walked into Shonda's apartment after receiving a desperate phone call. She told her she was sorry for everything and then hung up. Lily couldn't rest until she found out what was happening. When she opened the door to Shonda's apartment, using the key her part-

ner had given her, she saw Shonda was not alone. She was seated on a stool crying, while two men circled her. They had YBM jackets on, and it was apparent that they were there for business.

"I thought you said you lived alone?" one of them asked Shonda.

"I do. She's my partner."

"You really shouldn't have came here," one of them told Lily. "It was the worst decision in your life. Lock the door, Rook," he told the other man.

Lily was angry with herself now for leaving her weapon at home. "W-what's going on?"

"Your partner here didn't come through on a deal. We were gonna show the tape of her smokin' dope to the cops, but a few members of the YBM were also in the tape." He smacked her in the back of her head. "So Swoopes came up with a better idea."

"Please don't do that again," Lily requested, although she was disgusted by her partner's actions.

"Just what the fuck you goin' do?"

Lily was at a disadvantage.

"Just what I thought. Well, look, I'd like to draw this out, but we have something to do."

The other man grabbed Lily and was about to shoot her. She said, "Don't kill me."

"That's not possible," the leader said.

"Please don't kill me. If you don't, I'll kill her myself."

Shonda raised her head and looked at her partner. "What did you say?"

"You heard me!"

Heavy laughter filled the room.

"Hold fast. Did you just say you'd kill her yourself?"

Lily looked at Shonda and said, "Yes, if you let me go. You'll know if I didn't go through with it, and I'm sure you also know where to find me. This way you'll avoid a murder rap for killing a cop. I know you don't want that on your hands."

She was right. Killing a cop was serious; and if they were caught by other cops, they might not live to make it to trial.

"How do I know you won't snitch?" The leader walked over to Lily and looked down on her. Lily's eyes remained on Shonda's. The betrayal Shonda felt was unbearable.

"Because I know they can't protect me," she responded, looking up at him. *"They never could."* She focused back on Shonda.

"You smarter than I gave you credit for. Because you right, no one can protect you now." He walked away. *"Rook, let's let the officers get down to business."*

"You serious? What if Swoopes asks us what happened?"

The leader looked at the man and said, *"We'll tell him, it's all been taken care of."*

They moved toward the door. Right before he left, he looked back at Lily.

"I don't have to tell you to keep this between us. Because I know you know betta than to cross us." With that, they walked out.

Lily and Shonda stared at each other.

"So you gonna kill me?" Shonda asked, dropping her head again.

"*No. You gonna kill yourself. You dead, anyway. You made a decision without consulting me. And worst of all, I know what you did. It's the least you can do for me. It's the least you can do to make this right, and not make me kill you by my own hands.*"

"*You know about what I did?*"

"*I knew all along you had the waitress Jasmine killed. I overheard you talking on the phone to Katrina at Feeny's retirement party. What I didn't know was why. At first, I thought it was because you believed that Yvonna deserved to be off the street so bad that you were willing to do whatever you could to make it happen. But I caught up, and now I'm finding out that you're nothing more than a washed-up–ass dopehead.*"

"*I'm not using anymore. When I was, they found out I was a cop and taped me buying drugs from them. I don't even know how they found out. That shit was over five years ago. One day I come home to a letter from Swoopes telling me to meet him somewhere. He showed me the tape and blackmailed me. I guess they were waiting for the right time to use their card, and they did. But I've been clean for five years, Lily. I swear.*"

Lily was frustrated and wanted to get down to business. "*Where's your gun?*"

"*On the couch.*"

Lily walked toward the couch, grabbed the gun, and handed it to her.

"*Now do it.*"

Shonda cried loudly. "*I'm so sorry. Please forgive me.*"

After five more minutes of sobbing, and a prayer, Shonda placed the gun to her head and pulled the trig-

ger. Prior to her partner's killing herself, Lily felt that Shonda deserved to die because she dishonored the badge; but it didn't make her feel any better.

Lily had to live with feeling that Yvonna really should be punished.

She had to live with members of the YBM knowing about their agreement, and the possibility of them using it against her in the future.

And she had to live with not being strong enough to fight against the YBM to save her partner's life.

And then Lily realized that a system that would let a certified person go free could do nothing to protect her.

Back At Lily's

The officers are on their fourth glass.

"Wow. I can't believe it," Samuels says.

"It's all true."

"Well, we certainly have to tell someone," Jensen decides.

Lily looks at him and laughs. "You won't do that."

"Why wouldn't we? I want no part of this bullshit."

"Because if you do, she'll get away with everything else you're trying to book her for. They'll comb through this case so much, you won't have one."

"We can't just let this information sit!" Jensen says, yelling.

"We can and we *will*. It's the only way!" Lily laughs hysterically.

"What's so damn funny?" Jensen asks.

"Because I've just invited you boys into my private hell. How does it feel?"

They look at each other. "So what's the plan?"

"If we're gonna do this, we have to do it smart."

" 'We'?"

"Yes. I've decided to help you. I got this shit off my chest."

"So now what?"

"We have to be smarter than she is, and, believe me, she's smart. I didn't always realize that or accept that, but she is very bright. And you haven't been in the presence of evil *until* you've been around her." They look at each other and silently agree, having met her before. "And we'll need more people to help us."

"Who would get involved in this bullshit?" Samuels asks.

"You'd be surprised."

"Since you know so much, we're told that she kills people she seeks revenge on," Jensen states. "So who do you think she's after next?"

"Since Bernice Santana and Treyana are dead, I'd say Jhane, because Swoopes is in jail. And to tell you the truth, for his part in this shit, I wouldn't mind if she killed his ass." Lily is angry. "And you might want to offer Jhane protection until this blows over."

"We offered Jhane protection and she refused."

"That's mighty dumb." She pauses. "But I feel like I'm missing somebody else."

"Well, you said you testified against her. How you know she isn't after you?" Samuels asks.

"I don't know. And I don't know that she isn't after you either."

Both men swallow hard. "Well, who else?"

Lily paces her filthy floor in circles.

"Who am I missing?" She taps her chin. "Who is it?" She suddenly stops in her place. "Oh—oh . . . Cream Justice! Where is Cream Justice?"

Catch a Dead Man
by His Toes

It had been a warm night when Gabriella crept inside Jhane's home a few days back in Washington, D.C. She let herself in through the garage door Jhane had left open. Once inside, she carefully removed ten tampons from the open box and pierced a tiny hole through the plastic, using a syringe, dampening the cotton with the liquid Drano. She hoped she'd be around to see her ass scream when it was time to use them.

Now Gabriella sits impatiently outside of Jhane's house in a rental car. It was Thursday, and Jhane always ate at Olive Garden, her favorite restaurant. But where was she now? She needed to follow her to carry out another part of her nasty plan.

"How's the trip?" Jhane asks Jesse as she plops down onto her favorite green recliner. The chair rocks back and forth, making a squeaky sound. "Is Mexico beautiful?"

"Oh, Auntie Jhane! I can't explain how pretty it is here. I wish you were here with me." Her voice echoes from the speakerphone.

"I'm just happy you're there."

"Thank you for sending me. I really didn't think we'd be able to afford it. I mean, I know you've been struggling with me going to Duke and all the lessons."

"You deserve the best. *Owww*," she says, rubbing her chest.

"Is everything okay, Auntie Jhane?"

"Oh yeah, everything's fine." She falls back, settling into the softness of the recliner, and tries to push the pain she's feeling out of her mind. It's so unbearable that she doesn't think she'll be able to conceal it from Jesse. "Well, let me go grab a bite. Anyway, you should be enjoying Mexico, not wasting time talking to me."

"Where are you going? To Olive Garden?"

She laughs. "You know me too well!"

"Hey, Auntie," Jesse says, then pauses. "Um, have you seen her?"

"No. The police wanted me to have security here, but I refused. I'm not afraid of her anymore."

"Are you sure?"

"Yes, I'm sure. Now stop worrying about me and enjoy the rest of your trip."

"Okay, Auntie, I love you."

"And I love you more than you could ever know."

When Jhane ends the call, she allows her weight to fall deeply into the soft recliner. After all these years Jhane had allowed Jessse to think that the blood they shared didn't extend past niece and aunt.

They are so much more. They are mother and daughter. But Jesse isn't her only child. She also gave birth to Yvonna, and a very deep, dark secret surrounded their births. In the past, Jhane used drugs. She'd seen so many things—and did much more—and enjoyed medicating her pain away.

Jhane reaches down into the corner of her recliner and feels for her blue leather heroin kit. She places it on her lap and looks up at the ceiling.

"I'm trying to be a better person. I hope you know that."

After she lies to herself, she inserts the needle into her arm and sits back, allowing the heroin to control her. She feels a wave of euphoria and suddenly she could care less about her niece, her daughter, or any other relative, for that matter.

She sits in that recliner for thirty minutes, without moving. And when her high disintegrates, she's dropped back into her pitiful world. In an unbalanced state she stands up and moves to the bathroom. Once inside, she flops down on top of the toilet and spreads her beefy legs. Yellow urine escapes her body before turning red soon after.

She has gotten her period. Opening the cabinet under the sink, she removes a tampon and pushes the poison deeply inside.

"No problem, ma'am. I'll take care of that for you right away!"

The small waitress walks away to fill Jhane's usual order at the Olive Garden. But little does she know, extra Parmesan isn't the only thing she'll be eating. When the waitress leaves the kitchen fifteen minutes later with Jhane's meal in hand, she's stopped by Gabriella. Dressed in a formfitting one-piece jean outfit, she is far from being inconspicuous.

"Excuse me," Gabriella says, placing a hand on her shoulder. "That isn't for the woman over there, is it?"

The young white waitress, with red hair, says, "Yes, it is."

"Great! Let me take that for you. She's a good friend of mine."

"I'm sorry I can't do that." She looks Gabriella up and down, and smiles as she studies her body. "You're beautiful and glowing."

Picking up the wrong meaning of her inquisitive stare, she says, "This is Versace, honey! And trust me, it'll take more than slinging sauce rings around here before you'll ever be able to afford something as fly as this."

"I was only giving you a compliment!"

"And I'm giving you some advice."

"Ma'am, I have to get back to work." Her lips stop flapping when she sees the one-hundred-dollar bill Gabriella is waving.

Mr. Benjamin Franklin does seem to have that effect on them. Gabriella snatches the plate and gives her the money. "Now be gone." When the waitress doesn't move fast enough, Gabriella stomps her Prada pump and yells, "Shooo! Shooo! I've got work to do."

When the scrawny waitress leaves her sight, she walks to a table in the back, which is out of view from the business of the restaurant. Then she removes the paper bag from her purse. Next she pours the dandruff, dirt, and hair pile she collected from the dopehead into Jhane's meal. Next she grabs the oregano and Parmesan cheese jars from the table and shakes them like two maracas over her food to disguise the mess. Realizing she can't bring her the food and then expect her to eat it, she stops a male waiter.

"Hey, handsome."

"Hello. Are you okay? Do you need anything?"

"Actually, I do," she says, holding the plate like it is a pizza. "Do you mind taking this plate to my friend over there? I have to rush to the restroom."

"Of course not!" he says, blushing. He is extra considerate and she doesn't know why. In fact, everyone has been so nice to her lately that it has bugged the hell out of her. He is just about to walk the plate over to Jhane when he sees a small hair that wasn't concealed with enough oregano and Parmesan. "I'm gonna take this back. There's a hair in it."

"Don't worry about it. She doesn't mind."

He laughs and says, "You're kidding, right?"

She leans in and whispers heavily so that he can hear and read her lips. "Listen, fuck boy. I said she doesn't mind. Now go take the fuckin' plate!"

He hesitantly takes the plate and looks at her in horror. Arriving at the table, he places the food down, saying something to her before running off. Gabriella hides, in case he is ratting her out. But when Jhane takes heaping spoonful after heaping spoonful of the spaghetti and swallows, a smile spreads across Gabriella's face.

When her phone vibrates, she looks at it and sees it's a text message from Ming:

I come back from China next week. I have great news! Will share when I return. And yes, you can stay with me as long as you need.

Gabriella is irritated because she's running out of money and can no longer use the credit cards, because they are stolen, and the hotels she likes are expensive.

Focusing back on Jhane, she says, "Eat up, you greedy, fat bitch!" Placing nastiness in her food and poison in her tampons were just small ways of getting revenge. The real prize would come, once she killed her.

The moment thoughts of Jhane dying enter her

mind, Jhane moves around uncomfortably on her chair. *Did you get your period?* She hopes. *Did you use them toxic-filled tampons?* Jhane attempts to readjust herself by tugging at the seat of her pants. She even takes a few more bites of her spaghetti. That is, until her face bears a grimacing stare. She's in excruciating pain.

"Are you okay, ma'am?" a lady asks next to her.

"I . . . uh . . . don't know. I—I feel hot. My skin burns."

"Want me to call for help?"

Jhane stands and places a hand on her back. "I—I don't think so." She then doubles over. "I have to go."

Jhane runs outside, and Gabriella is laughing so hard that she feels a fluttering sensation in her stomach. Gabriella follows, trying to maintain at least a ten-foot distance. Jhane can't stand up straight during the entire walk to her car.

"You are so beautiful," a white woman says, looking at Gabriella's body.

"I know, bitch, now move. You in my way."

The woman holds her mouth open in shock and walks off.

Gabriella decides that she must see where Jhane's going. But she changes her mind when she sees the two cops she can't fucking stand walking toward the restaurant. She backs up, spots a wooden phone booth, and hides inside. The male waiter, whom she punked earlier, sees her hurrying away seconds before the officers approach him.

"Excuse me, son," Officer Jensen says. "Can we talk to you for a minute?"

"Am I in trouble?"

"I don't know. It depends on what you tell us."

The waiter's face turns red. "O—okay." He swallows hard.

"Have you seen this woman? Someone said they saw someone fitting her description come in here."

The man looks at the picture and looks behind him in Gabriella's direction. Out of view of the officers, she runs her finger across her neck in a slicing motion.

The terrified, young waiter swallows hard again, turns back around, and looks at the officers. "No, sir, I haven't seen her."

"Are you sure, son? You seem out of it."

"Yes, sir. I'm sure. I haven't seen her before."

"Well, if you do, take this card and call me." The officer hands it to him. "It's really important, son. This woman is dangerous."

When they leave the restaurant, Gabriella hangs back awhile. She knows now that it will be difficult finishing her list, but she has no intention of stopping until she is done. "It's gonna take more than that to stop me, bitches. Way more."

Scary Kinda Love

Peter and Guy are at their desks waiting for Cheryl's call. When the phone doesn't ring after two hours of waiting, Peter decides to call her, instead.

"Have you gotten any of the fingerprints back?" Jensen asks.

"You have to be patient." Irritation is heavy in her voice.

"And I told you that case is important and that I need it now! A lot of people have been showing up missing and her doctor says she hasn't been to any of her appointments or taking her medicine." Silence.

"Please don't call me, bothering me at work. I'm tired of this little game, and you have to wait just like the others."

He clears his throat and walks away from his desk in case Guy overheard the conversation and became aware of his lies. In front of his partner, he portrayed himself to be the man, when he was far from it.

"What do you mean?"

"You have been harassing me ever since I left you, and I'm tired of it, Peter. Now I will show you respect, but only as it relates to our business relationship."

The phone is sweaty and wet from his body temperature rising. When he first met her, she was timid and afraid of him. Now she's acting like he never beat her a day in her life.

"Peter? Peter? Are you there?"

"Listen, slut! I'm still the man you knew, and don't for one moment think you left me. I let you go because if I wanted you dead, you would be. Now . . . I sucked your pussy dry every night we were together for over a year. Whether I wanted to or not, and most nights I didn't. Now I'm asking for your help. Are you going to help me or not?"

Silence.

"Peter Jensen, I want you in my office first thing in the morning," a male voice demands.

Peter is so shocked from hearing her boss's voice that he almost drops the phone. Although he doesn't report to him directly, he outranks Peter, and a complaint from him carries weight.

"Yes . . . sir."

"Good! And just so you know, I ran the finger-prints personally. We'll deal with both matters to-morrow."

Peter hangs up and stares into space.

"Peter . . . what she say?" Guy asks, walking over to him. "Are the results back or not?"

Peter can't speak. He is realizing that this case is already taking more from him than he is willing to give.

Taxicab Confessions

"Where are you going, young lady?" the taxi driver asks Gabriella, studying her in the rearview mirror. His Jamaican accent is thick, despite speaking very clear English.

"I'm going to 6745 Old Marlboro Pike." She gives an address in the vicinity, but not the exact one.

"You got it," he says, taking a look at her beauty again. "How was your night?"

"Well, let's see. I tried to kill somebody today, but the cops came, so I couldn't finish her off. And now it's going to put a dent in everything else."

"Oh . . . really?" His eyebrows rise and he thinks she's joking. "You too pretty to be a murderer."

"Trust me," she says, crossing her legs and leaning back. She adjusts her shirt a little to get more comfortable. "There are a lot of pretty killers out there."

"And why do you kill?"

"Because I can. Why do you drive people around like a slave?" she says, looking into the mirror at him. " 'Cause you can."

He frowns and she smiles.

"You can't find anything better to do with your time?"

"No, there's nothing more liberating than taking a life."

"You sound serious."

"Who said I wasn't?"

He looks at her and then back at the road.

"We're here." He can't wait to get her crazy ass out of his car.

She opens the door and eases out. "If you wait, I'll let you set your own tip."

"Sure." The moment her feet hit the curb, he pulls off.

Scccuuurrr!

Gabriella looks behind her and laughs before hiking the two long blocks up the dark street leading to Bradshaw's house. Her stomach flutters again and it's starting to irritate her. She rubs it a little and keeps walking. She hates depending on others and needing somewhere to stay. But what else can she do? All her money is gone, and Penny would send her up the long road if she stepped foot back on her property. Bradshaw is her only hope.

Once at Bradshaw's house, she walks up the large stairs of his townhome. And when she is one step away from his front door, she glances into the window, which is opened up a crack, and sees the movie company officials who have tried to get her story.

"Tim and Mora!" she says out loud.

They are sitting on the couch, listening to a small tape recorder they have connected to speakers. And then . . . she hears her own voice: "Yeah, me and Yvonna. I think people just need to let us be. We might not be like everyone thinks we should be, but we're real. I'm real. And we don't need no medicine to change us."

He had a tape recorder in his jean pockets when he came to visit her, and she didn't know it. Bradshaw was careful about making sure that his jeans remained on the bed the entire time they spoke and made love. From the moment he met her in the doctor's office, he had ulterior motives—to gain information on her story that the court reports couldn't provide.

They really wanted the details from her; but after they propositioned Yvonna and she refused, they sent Bradshaw. In fact, the phone number he gave her was provided by the movie company. It was a setup. Everything.

Bradshaw has been so dead set on doing whatever he has to do to get the money necessary to get his daughter back that he didn't take time to realize who he was fucking with. He thought Yvonna was *faking* crazy—like he did, to dodge murder charges. Behind her back, to the movie representatives, he praised how great her acting skills were and commented on how she even had him participate in overcoming the Gabriella personality.

Perhaps if he'd realized the severity of her situation, he would've packed up and moved out of town rather than cross her. Bradshaw is making a grave mistake, and he doesn't even know it.

Seeing and hearing his treachery causes her to stumble backward, grabbing the rail before falling to the ground.

"I shoulda known you were nothin' more than a fuckin' liar!" Gabriella curses into the night air. "You better be glad I don't have my gun."

Feeling like she needs to do something now, she picks up one of the large gray stones in his yard and throws it against his living-room window. *Crash!* She runs down the stairs and hides.

"What was that?" Bradshaw asks as the crew follows him.

"I don't know," Tim answers.

Brad looks around.

"Have any enemies?" they joke.

"Not that I know of."

"Well, let's get back in and finish this story. You're about to become a rich man."

They go inside, but he remains outside, scanning the grounds. When Gabriella sees he's alone, she steps out and shows herself.

"You're a dead man," she tells him in a calm

voice. "I told you not to fuck with me, but you didn't get it."

He is so stunned that he doesn't move for two minutes.

"You should've checked my rep, because you fucked with the wrong bitch."

After that, she walks away. Her steps go from walking to running. She's angry for allowing herself to feel something for another human being. But she makes a promise to never let it happen again.

Ever.

Change of Heart

"We know you heard from her by now. She didn't just disappear off the face of the earth," Peter says.

"Are you sure? I mean . . . ya said you haven't found her."

"Don't be smart!"

"Well, it's true. And I ain't gotta tell you shit, even if I *did* know where she was. So unless you chargin' me with somethin', I suggest ya leave me alone!" Penny yells at the top of her lungs on the steps of her house.

Peter is quiet and observes what she *isn't* saying more than what she *is* saying. Her eyes tell him she cares about Yvonna.

"Penny, why are you protecting her?" He looks upon her dark, wrinkled face.

"I'm not protectin' nobody."

"I think you are. You called the police a while

back saying someone was in your house. Who was it? Was it Yvonna?"

"If I knew 'em, dey wouldn't have been strangers, now would dey?"

"Look, we're here to solve a case," Guy intrudes. "We don't mean to be rude. If we are, I apologize."

The anger is wiped clean from her face.

"You said she stayed here awhile. Do you mind if we see the room where she stayed? We won't be long," Guy asks.

Peter looks at him as if he's stupid. In his mind, if the woman wasn't willing to help, why would she allow them into her home?

"Sure," Penny says, opening the door wide. "Come on inside."

They didn't know that Penny cleaned the basement from top to bottom and was not concerned about them finding anything, anyway. Although she didn't believe in the murder of innocent people, she also didn't believe Yvonna was in her right frame of mind. Penny still wanted to help her.

"Wow," Guy says, looking around. "Smells real clean, doesn't it?"

"Yeah, *too* clean," Peter adds, looking over the neat basement.

They move around a few items, pictures, and shoes that Yvonna had left behind. They even look under the bed and around Penny's workbench. Still, they find nothing.

"Let's go. She's cleaned this place spotless. We won't find anything here."

"That's why she let us in. Well, let me go drop off the kids in the pool," Peter says, moving into the tiny pink bathroom, where he plans on taking a shit.

Plopping down on the toilet, he pulls out his cell phone and looks at the screen. He was supposed to go to meet Chief Walker earlier that morning, but he didn't go. He figures the damage is done and he should focus on bringing Yvonna into custody. He reasons he doesn't need to see the fingerprint results to know Yvonna is guilty. He's not even looking for other suspects—even though Yvonna has not been formally charged. As it stands now, the only thing she is wanted for is missing her court-ordered doctor appointments with Jona, and he is using this as a means to break the law.

After straining and releasing shit into the bowl, he exhales, flushes, and stands up. He is just about to leave without washing his hands or his ass, until he turns around and looks at the small commode.

"I wonder," he says aloud, with his balls dangling and his shit spinning in the toilet.

He lifts the top off the toilet tank and removes a plastic bag with a black journal inside. "I knew it!"

After getting himself together, he rushes outside, eager to show his revelation to his partner. If she wrote anything incriminating in the journal, he is sure he'd have a case. The only problem is, he doesn't have a warrant.

Must Know

Gabriella sits in a wheelchair, wearing a big, ugly black wig and large glasses. She'd gotten her hands on some oversized jeans and a large gray shirt, which she placed wet stains across. Leaning to the side, she looks like she is suffering from a body-debilitating disease; and that was her intent. The more docile she appears, the more harmless she appears. And the more harmless, the greater chance she would have that they'd leave her the fuck alone. She even has a clear cup in her hand, which she filled with soapy water to represent spit.

"Hello, ma'am. Do you need any help?" a nurse asks. Gabriella is only a few feet from Jhane's door. To prevent her voice from being detected, she shakes her head no.

"You're sure?" the nurse asks, bending down and placing her hand gently on Gabriella's knee.

Again she nods yes, a little more roughly this time.

" 'Cause I don't mind taking you to where you have to go."

Gabriella sits up and says, "Look, bitch! I said I'm fine! Now beat it!"

The nurse backs into the wall, looks down at Gabriella, and walks hurriedly down the hallway.

Damn! How many times do a bitch got to shake her head no?

When the nurse is out of sight, Gabriella goes back into meek mode and rolls herself inside Jhane's room. It does her heart good to see Jhane hooked up to all types of machines. Although she has to admit, she didn't think soaking Jhane's tampon with liquid Drano would cause such a major problem. Once she is fully inside the room, she pulls the curtain to conceal them.

"Look at you. You're a pitiful-looking bitch." Gabriella laughs.

Jhane's eyes are closed and her head is turned in the opposite direction. Gabriella walks around the bed and looks at her face. When she gets closer, she stoops down and smacks Jhane so hard that her lips tremble. Loving the way her skin feels under her fingers, Gabriella smacks her again. And again. And again . . . until her lips bleed.

When she stops, Jhane opens her eyes and says, "Are you done?"

Gabriella is shocked at her response and that

she took blow after blow without flinching. "You were up the entire time?"

"Are . . . you . . . done?" she repeats, pronouncing each word clearly.

Gabriella steps back. "I don't know if I'm done, bitch," she says, getting her gumption back. "Give me a second and I might hit your ass again."

"The officers told me someone spotted you following me in the restaurant. Is it true?"

"What do you think?"

"Yvonna, I'm sorry." She looks at her. "I'm sorry for hurting you. I really am. I know you don't believe me. And to be honest, I don't expect you to. But . . . I was young when I got pregnant with you. And there are many things . . . many, many things that you don't know about."

"Pregnant with me? Fuck are you talking about?"

"You are my child. And because of circumstances, which I can't explain in detail, I hated *them*. I hated all of *them* for forcing me to give you up. I fought *them* so *hard*, Yvonna." Tears roll out of her eyes and onto the pillow behind her head. She looks at the ceiling. "But *they* are heartless. *They* have control over everything, even my sister. I know you don't believe me, but I really did fight to get you back, and even was going to tell someone about *them*. But *they* promised if I did, *they'd* make my life a living hell. I didn't know how to get over the pain, but *they* showed me. *They* introduced me to drugs"—she looks back at Gabriella—"and I loved it. Before long, *they* managed to convince me that you were evil and that everything I experienced was *your* fault. After a while, I was happy to give you up and hated you every day in the process."

"I don't understand what the fuck you're telling us! This doesn't make any fucking sense!" Gabriella grows loud, not thinking about who might hear her.

"I'm *your mother.* You're *my daughter. You and Jesse both.* You were born into something that we couldn't get out of. The pain I felt whenever looking at you cut me so deep that I bailed out on you, and I was wrong."

Gabriella takes four steps back until her legs give out and her body drops onto a yellow chair against the wall, by the windowsill.

"I was so wrong, and I'm finally realizing it now. I was a coward."

Gabriella is suddenly gone, and it is Yvonna who sits in the room with Jhane. Her mind wanders over what was just said. She remembers it all. She immediately goes back to the day Jesse was shot and taken to the hospital.

The day Jesse was shot

Thirty minutes later, Jhane rushed into the hospital to speak to the doctors. When Yvonna stood up to greet her, Jhane looked at her coldly.

"*Get the fuck away from me, bitch!*" *Jhane told her*

with her fist balled up. "When Jesse pulls through, she's staying with me. I don't care what you say or that deadbeat father of yours says." She walked off to talk to the doctors.

"Don't worry about her." Sabrina gripped her.

"Yeah! She's just upset at what's happening with Jesse," Cream added.

Yvonna didn't want to say anything, but Jhane's attitude toward her hurt, but she was going to play it off. Fuck my family, *Yvonna thought.* I got my girls and they got me! And when my sister gets betta, the three of dem will be all I care about.

Yvonna looks up at Jhane and says, "If I'm your daughter, why would you hurt me so badly?"

"Because you reminded me of my failures. You reminded me of *them.* At that point in my life, I had escaped and couldn't risk going back. *They* warned me to be careful, and *they* watched my every move. *They* still do."

"Who are 'they'? And what do 'they' got to do with me?"

"Yvonna, I can't say a lot. It's for your own protection. I just want you to know that I was an awful mother. And trust me, I'm getting everything I deserve."

Yvonna's very confused and can't seem to wrap her tortured mind around everything that Jhane is saying, so she focuses on what she wants to know most of all.

"Who are the people who raised me?"

"She isn't your mother, and he isn't your father."

Yvonna feels like she's on the verge of a nervous breakdown, and she drinks the water in Jhane's cup. "Well, who were they? I need to know what's going on!"

"I'm sorry, I can't say much more."

"Well, why fuckin' tell me, if you won't tell me everything?" she asks as tears fall down her face.

"Because I'm dying from breast cancer. It's progressing rapidly and they don't think I'll make it past a few days."

Yvonna is quiet—and for some reason she's hurt.

"Yvonna, please come here." Jhane reaches out to her.

Yvonna stands and walks up to her.

"Before I die, I want you to know that I've always loved you. Even when I felt I didn't. The more I hated you, the more I realized my love. Hate and love are closely related, Yvonna. And when you have your baby, you'll understand that sometimes you don't make the right decisions, although you mean to. And I made the worst mistakes in my life, and most of them before I was old enough to know what was going on. Your health problem is my fault." Yvonna looks away and Jhane pulls her hand. "Look at me, Yvonna." She does. "It's all my fault. Jesse loves you. And if she sees you trying, she'll be by your side. You two need each other, but she's scared and got to know she's safe around you. Let the hospital help."

In that moment Jhane gives something to Yvonna that she always wanted: a mother's love. Although there are still many, many unanswered questions, for the second that Jhane recognizes her wrongs, Yvonna feels euphoric. And then Yvonna realizes she won't have her in her life. She realizes that Jhane will die soon, and again she'll be alone. She doesn't understand why everybody she cares about—everyone she ever loved—is taken from her. She hates life and curses God for bringing her into the world.

Now she's angry and feels motions in her stomach. Her head is spinning. Like it has many times before, hate consumes her. She snatches her hand away.

"I hope you rot in hell, you fat, ugly bitch. And because I don't trust your fate to cancer, I'm gonna make sure death happens to you now."

Yvonna snatches the pillow from up under Jhane's neck, takes the finger monitor off Jhane's hand, which the doctor used to check the pressure, and places it on her own to prevent the nurses from detecting something is wrong. Next she presses the shallow pillow over Jhane's face. Jhane's legs and arms kick and jerk, but Yvonna maintains her pressure, pushing harder and harder into the bed.

"Die, bitch! Die!" She is crying and yelling. "Fucking die!"

And when Jhane stops moving, Yvonna removes the pillow from her face and places it back under her head. She looks down at Jhane's lifeless body. This is the first time she's been so close to her; she immediately recognizes their resemblance. *You were my mother.* Now she hates herself and Jhane even more—not to mention she left her with so many unanswered questions. "Death looks good on you."

Yvonna slides the pressure monitor off her finger, hops back in the wheelchair, and pushes herself out the door. The nurses and hospital aides rush toward Jhane's room, missing Yvonna by seconds.

It is the happy ending she always wanted.

No Involvement

"Do you mind if I have a seat?"

"What is this about?" Terrell Shines asks as he looks at Jona Maxwell. He is seated at his desk in his office.

"I've been calling you, but you stopped answering my calls. Is there a reason?"

"Jona Maxwell?" This is the first time they'd met in person.

"Yes." She sits down without waiting for him to offer.

"Look . . . I have an appointment in a few minutes. I'm gonna need you to leave."

"Sir, we really need your help. Please. Just a few moments."

Terrell walks around his desk and sits on the edge of it. Folding his arms against his muscular chest, he looks down at her and she's intimidated.

Now she understands how her patients feel. Not only is she taken by how attractive he is, she is also taken by his elusiveness. She is trained to read minds, but she failed when it came to reading men. She is so bad at it that she hasn't fucked in over two years.

"What do you need?"

"Yvonna has gotten worse. And I don't know if you've been looking at the news, but there are several people dead who have had contact with her in the past, and several others are missing. Now I know you two had a relationship, and you might feel uncomfortable helping us, but we need you."

"We?"

"Yes, there are quite a few of us."

He laughs. "What is this? A task force?"

"Sort of. Right now, she's really only wanted for questioning and for missing her appointments with me. The last information we had on her, she was in the hospital for an injury to her hand. No one has been able to reach her since."

"I've given up trying to help Yvonna. And to be honest, I'm not sure why whenever her name comes up, people come to me. She was my fiancée, not my patient. I only helped her out when she needed me and then she ran off with that Dave person." He sounds bitter, like he's still in love; Jona is slightly jealous.

When he sits down, she observes the pictures against his wall. In all of them he is alone; for some reason she is pleased, because she thinks he's single. Jona is angry with herself for choosing such a modest-looking outfit. She looks like someone's mother instead of a single, horny woman.

"Terrell, I beg you to reconsider."

"Leave now."

Jona drops her head, pushes her chair back, and stands up. Walking over to his desk, she reaches into her purse, removes the list Yvonna created, and places it on his desk. Then she jots down an address on his notepad and puts it down.

"That's a list she created recently." She closes her purse and places it on her arm. "And we're all going to be there tomorrow night, if you want to come. Enjoy the rest of your day," she says, looking up for a minute to see his face.

"Good-bye, Dr. Maxwell." For some reason she takes his shortness personally.

"Good-bye." She turns around and walks hurriedly toward the door. It looks like their plan would have to be worked out, minus one doctor.

Time Is Now

"What is your problem, Peter? Your gotdamn ass out there threatenin' female officers, and shit!" Lieutenant Michael Cronnell yells.

"Sir, I'm trying to solve this case."

"I want this case solved too, but you're out there on some gotdamn personal bullshit! I suggest you back off! 'Cause you're five seconds from findin' yourself in the unemployment line. And about that blonde, it's over. Don't go within two feet of her or the only thing you gonna be fuckin' is me! Am I clear?"

"Yes, sir," Jensen says, embarrassed at receiving the lieutenant's outburst.

Without waiting for any more comment, Cronnell slides a manila folder across the officer's desk. "This came for you!" Cronnell storms away.

"Peter, what's goin' on?" Guy finally asks. He

didn't dare speak while his boss was there, for fear he'd receive some of the backlash too.

Peter ignores him and opens the results. When he does, the wind is knocked out of his body.

"What is it, Peter?" Guy asks, standing up. "What the fuck is it?"

Light Jogging

Bradshaw is jogging down his street for his daily five-mile run. With the money he is getting from the movie company, he is on top of the world. And he'd already made arrangements to get the in-house security necessary to get custody of his daughter. Thoughts of betraying Yvonna do cross his mind, but he can't take her seriously. Because if his daughter's social workers found out that he was dealing with someone like Yvonna, he would have been deemed unfit and would have lost her for the rest of his life. It would have never worked.

"Looking good, Mr. Hughes," a white woman yells as he jogs by. She has been sweet on him ever since he moved to the Upper Marlboro area earlier in the year. "Need help with that tight, little bun of yours?"

"How 'bout I join you for some coffee later," he tells her.

"Coffee" meant joining her, like he often did, for a morning fuck session.

"I'll get a pot brewing."

He winks and jogs on his way. The moment he reaches a group of trees at the bottom of the hill, he sees a woman smiling at him in a red Toyota 4Runner. He recognizes her immediately.

"There he goes!" Gabriella says to her.

Realizing the only person she had in her life was Gabriella, Yvonna has stopped trying to fight what *was* and just let things *be*. Gabriella would always be a part of her life, and she likes it because it made her stronger.

"I see his fucking ass!"

He quickly scans his surroundings to see where he can run, but it's too late. She already presses the gas pedal, running smack-dab into his body, knocking him to the ground. It's difficult to run over him at first, but she builds up enough momentum to push the large stolen truck over his limbs. His body trails under her truck for about a half mile before eventually falling off.

"Dead men speak no tales," Yvonna says.

"Not even for a movie deal." Gabriella laughs.

Sick and Fucking Tired

Using the money she'd stolen from an elderly man she carjacked for his truck, she checked into a hotel in D.C. She knew she couldn't stay long, because her cash was low, and she knew Ming would be coming back to America soon. Yvonna has texted her friend the name of the hotel she is currently staying at, and Ming replied that she is more than happy to make a space for her in her large eight-bedroom house in Bowie.

Yvonna has been suffering from depression so bad that all she wants to do lately is eat, sleep, and cry. Revenge is always great, but at this point she needs more. She needs love.

Sitting on the bed, she pulls out a large sweater from her shopping bag. It is three sizes too big for her and swallows her body. She's gained so much weight around her stomach, ass, and thighs that she's begun to hate her body. Easing into the sweater, she throws on some sweatpants, ready to watch TV, when there is a knock on the door.

She opens it. "Oh, my goodness!" Yvonna yells looking at Ming. She missed her friend a lot.

"Don't act like you miss me, bitch. Who you got in here fucking?" Ming, wearing a long fur coat, looks around. Her face is full.

"It's not even that kind of party."

Ming takes her coat off, revealing a large, protruding belly. Yvonna's mouth drops.

"Ming, you're fat!"

"No! I'm pregnant. You're fat!" she says, looking at the large sweater. "You don't dress same. Why?" she asks, pointing at her body. "Fuck you been doing?"

"Long story," Yvonna says, depressed. "But who is the father?"

"You not believe," Ming answers in her broken English. Her breasts are larger and she even has a nice ass. Pregnancy becomes her.

"I don't know. . . . Choy . . . Ho . . . Hung? Who? Just tell me, bitch!"

"Bradshaw, the man we fucked in threesome when I in town!" she says excitedly.

Yvonna can't believe Ming got pregnant by him, especially after she left his body earlier for dead. "And you kept it?"

"Why not? Me want black baby, me keep black baby." She rubs her stomach and speaks as if it's some kind of nigger doll.

Suddenly Yvonna is jealous because she realizes that for the rest of Ming's life, she'll always have someone to care for her. Yvonna can't say the same about herself.

"What's wrong, my friend?"

"Nothing." Yvonna is lying.

"You sure?"

"Yes."

"Wanna get high?" Ming asks, retrieving a joint from her purse.

"I thought you weren't supposed to smoke while you're pregnant."

"Girl, please! This baby might as well know early that Ming gets fucked up!"

They laugh and enjoy each other's company. For the first time, in a long time, Yvonna smiles.

Now What?

Jona Maxwell, Lily Alvarez-Martin, Guy Samuels, and Peter Jensen sit in a quiet conference room in a Hyatt hotel.

"I don't understand. How could Cream's fingerprints be on the electric panel instead of Yvonna's?" Jona continues.

"I don't know either, but we probably won't find out for a while," Peter says.

"Where is Cream? She just seemed to drop off the face of the earth," Guy adds.

"If Yvonna had anything to do with it, she probably did," Lily comments. She has gained a little weight since sharing her secret about her partner.

"Did they get a match on the fingerprints from the Bernice Santana case?" Jona asks, having nothing much to contribute other than random questions.

"Yes. Bernice Santana was murdered by the victim they found her with. His name was Andrew Whinston, and they're saying he killed himself and her."

"What about Crystal Baisley? A witness saw a woman fitting Yvonna's description taking a knife out of her body, on the side of the road, in broad daylight." Jona continues trying her best to be sure that no stones are left unturned.

"I know. But they found the knife not too far from the crime scene and tested the prints. They belonged to a Cole Warren. They caught up with him and he was in a drug-induced daze. For days he couldn't even remember his own name."

"And Jhane?" Jona hesitates.

"She had cancer and died of natural causes."

Jona frantically looks around the room. It finally has sunk in. Yvonna could do whatever she wants, to whomever she wants. "She's getting away with it. She's killing everybody she wants and is getting away with it! We're next!" Jona suddenly cries out.

The room is silent. They all saw the list Jona had shown them not too long ago with their names on it. They know their fate is coming soon.

"I don't know why y'all thought we could kill this bitch by conventional means. We'll never get her if we try to do things the *right* way," Lily asserts. Once the weaker one, she had quickly become one of the strongest out of the group.

"She's right, but we don't have to become victims. I have someone I want you all to meet," Peter says, getting up to open the door. But when he does, instead of seeing his surprise guest, in walks Terrell. After seeing his name on the list, and being aware of Yvonna's capabilities, he has decided to join the group.

"Thanks for coming," Jona says.

He doesn't respond and finds a seat amongst the other walking dead. Not wanting him to feel uncomfortable just yet, Peter continues his presentation.

"We have to fight back if we wanna survive," Peter states. He goes to the door and motions for someone to come in. In walks a man whose six-foot-five frame is clearly in disguise. "Here is our answer. He's going to make our problem go away."

"About time! Now we're talking," Lily remarks, cheering at the sight.

Everyone, but Peter, looks at her as if she's crazy. "Are you suggesting we participate in murder?" Terrell questions.

"I'm suggesting that we survive."

Terrell grabs his keys and is preparing to leave, when Peter opens Yvonna's journal, which he stole from Penny's house. He reads a passage aloud: " 'And Terrell, that no-good–ass, limp-dick muthafucka is goin' pay for gettin' in my fuckin' business. He can't last a minute in the bedroom. Maybe when he's a stiff, his dick will stay hard and last." Peter closes the book when he's done.

Gary laughs a little, and Peter looks at Terrell.

Terrell's desire to live overcomes his embarrassment and he takes a seat.

"There's a passage in here about each one of you, including me. We have to kill this crazy bitch. She has chronicled most of her life in here, and I haven't been able to sleep since reading this thing. I couldn't enter this into evidence because I took it without a warrant. I'm playing her game now."

"And her doctors and lawyers would probably find some way to get it thrown out of court, anyway," Lily adds.

"So what do you wanna do?" the guest asks. He is so still and quiet they forgot he is in there.

"He'll murder her for ten grand. That's two thousand apiece. By paying him, we seal our pact and take back our lives. He'll even make it look like a murder/rape. What do you wanna do?" Peter looks around the room and sees everyone mentally weighing their options.

It is evident that it must've taken a supercrazy bitch to make two doctors and three cops conspire together in murder. But they have no other options, having tried everything they could. At the end of the day, their names are on her list; and lately she had won every game played.

One by one, they all agree, and they leave the rest in God's hands.

Bone Crusher

"Sir, sir . . . can you hear me?" a nurse asks Bradshaw as he lies in the bed, paralyzed from the neck down. "If you can hear me, blink your eyes." He blinks.

"Sir, you've been hurt very badly, and we're going to need you to help us help you." There are two cops present. "We're going to bring over a letter board. When you see the first letter you want to use to help us, blink." She brings over the letter board. "Blink now if you understand what I'm saying."

Blink.

"Do you know who did this?"

Blink.

"Great. Let's get started."

The nurse points at letter after letter, and the process seems to take twenty minutes. But, one by one, he blinks; and the nurse's expression changes from hopefulness to disappointment as each word is formed.

"Sir, are you sure?"

Blink.

"So you're going to let whoever did this just get away?"

Blink.

The officers exhale and throw their hands up in the air. "Well, if you change your mind, I'm sure you'll find a way to *blink* and let us know. We're out of here."

When they are gone, the nurse looks at what is spelled. It reads: *She will kill me and I don't want to die.*

"Whoever she is can't hurt you now."

A tear runs down his face hearing her lies.

Date with Death

Yvonna is removing her clothes after just recently leaving the free clinic in Southeast D.C. She has a lot of information to absorb and wants to get into the tub and relax, to let everything soak in. If she had a mother to explain her body, visiting the clinic would not have been necessary. Looking at her phone, she sees that Ming texted her to say she'd be picking her up in the morning to move into her house.

Every step she takes around the hotel room weighs on her, both mentally and physically. She has just removed her sweatpants and is wearing nothing outside of a large, comfortable black sweater and her panties. She hears a knock at the door and she yells, "Who is it?"

When she doesn't get an answer, she continues about the room, packing clothes and preparing for her bath. She is hoping whoever it is just went away, when she hears the knock again.

"Who is it?" she yells, her face contorted.

Feeling frustrated, she walks to the door and swings it open. When she does, she's met with a blow to her face and falls to the floor. "Who are you?" she screams as the tall masked man rushes toward her. "Why are you hurting me?"

He hits her over and over, and she begs for mercy. He has orders to make her case look personal, using assault and battery.

"Please, you're hurting us," she says. "Please stop."

Despite all the people she's killed, here she is begging for the mercy she never gave her victims. And just as she'd ignored their requests, the stranger was ignoring hers.

She manages to get up and runs for the door. He catches her and pulls her backward by her sweater, sending her feet and legs up in the air before she drops back to the floor again. He tries to grab her to finish his work, but she's using legs, arms, toes, knees, and every other body part she can. Yvonna is strong, and he's surprised.

It looks as if she might get away again, until he hits her so hard in her eye, she sees stars. Over and over again he beats her in the face with brute force. Yvonna's life and crimes suddenly flash before her eyes and she sees some of their faces. She is a killer; and she quickly comes to the realization that, like her victims, she must die.

When she has nothing left to fight him with, anyway, the man places his large hands around her throat, tightens, and squeezes. Her head turns to her left and she sees Gabriella beside her, lying faceup. She also looks weak. He squeezes tighter and tears roll off her face.

"I don't wanna die," Gabriella says softly. "I don't wanna die."

"It'll be okay." Yvonna smiles, and the man notices her calmness and squeezes her throat harder.

In all of his life, he never fought so hard to kill someone. There is a first for everything, but it isn't long before Yvonna sees a bright, calming light and closes her eyes.

*We not fucking around this time!
If you like the way the story ended, don't read the next page!*

*You just had to do it!
Fuck it! Read at your own
damn risk!*

I Ain't Goin' Be Able
to Do It

The hit man is still choking her, until she closes her eyes.

"Finally," he says, wiping the sweat off his head with the back of his hand.

But when he stands up, he musses up her sweater by mistake and her nine months' pregnant belly is exposed. He's overcome with immediate grief.

Fifty-year-old Charles Bank has been killing for over twenty years and has three rules: Never kill a child. Never kill an elderly person. And never kill a pregnant woman. He's just broken his own rule and is angry, believing he'll have bad luck.

He knows it's just a matter of seconds before she dies. So he picks up her body and places her carefully on the bed. He's angry at Peter for not telling him. He has no idea that Peter hasn't seen her in months.

Charles spends a few minutes conducting mouth-to-mouth resuscitation and is discouraged, until she coughs. She's alive! Yvonna looks at him and is too weak to be afraid. Still not sure she's out of the darkness, he leaves her there, drives a mile up the road, and calls the ambulance.

Thanks to Charles Bank, Yvonna Harris is alive and kicking.

Changed?

One year later

"What made her commit to your program?" Penny asks. She is accompanied by Jesse and Delilah, Yvonna's one-year-old daughter. They sit on comfortable cloth chairs in front of the doctor's desk. And Delilah tries repeatedly to grab a crystal baby bird off the doctor's desk.

"Excuse me," Penny says, cutting the doctor off before she speaks. "No, Delilah. Ya can't have that." She takes it from the baby's hands.

Yvonna had reached out to Penny last week and begged her to care for her daughter, Delilah, because she knew Penny would love her like her own, especially if Yvonna was trying to get help. That was something Penny had always wanted.

Penny gladly agreed to care for Delilah, until Yvonna finished the program in six months. Yvonna committed for many reasons, including not wanting the system to take her baby. After all, she had missed appointments with Jona and risked jail time. But no one but Penny ever *really* knew that Yvonna was still suffering from DID. And no one at all knew she had killed again.

Ming, Yvonna's best friend, had an attitude when Yvonna committed herself and gave Delilah to Penny. She wanted to care for Delilah. But Yvonna didn't think it was a good idea because she didn't even take great care of Boy, her own son, not to mention she was always going back and forth to China. Delilah's beautiful brown skin and rosy cheeks got attention wherever she roamed. Just like her mother, she was strikingly beautiful and already extremely smart.

"She says she committed herself for her own reasons."

"Can she leave at anytime now?" Jesse asks.

"Unfortunately not. Once they commit to our program, they must continue."

As the adults speak amongst themselves, Delilah continues to reach for the crystal bird.

"No, Delilah," Penny says firmly and lovingly. She removes the bird again from her hands. "It's not yours, so ya can't have it." Delilah cries; and she looks so cute, Penny is immediately remorseful.

"She's been doing really well, and this program is one of the best in the country for dissociative identity disorder." The doctor continues ignoring the baby altogether. "We had to design a special program for Yvonna, since her symptoms don't necessarily fit perfectly into the DID category," Dr. Connie Griswald advises.

"So who's payin' for this?"

"Her case is so unique that we were able to get funding, and her friend Ming picks up most of the other costs."

Penny and Jesse look at one another because they met Ming a month back and neither of them cared for her because they thought she was a bad influence.

"You seem optimistic, Doctor," Jesse states. "And I don't mean to be rude, but they said my sister was cured before. And since you accepted her as a patient, despite her having relapses, how can you be sure?" Jesse has grown into a beautiful young woman with a thriving career as a local singing artist. At the end of the day, unlike her sister, she is mostly boring.

"Well, we've been studying her thoroughly and we think we've managed to combine the personalities into one. We also know why she splits into personalities. She's been very cooperative, and it makes the process easier."

"Wait—you want to keep Gabriella?" Jesse questions.

"Not necessarily keep Gabriella, but there are some good qualities that Gabriella possesses. For instance, she's strong, vocal, and—"

"Evil," Penny interrupts. She looks at the doctor and then at Jesse. "Oh, I'm sorry."

They laugh. "Don't be sorry," Jesse says. "You and I both know how dangerous Gabriella can be."

"I understand why you're concerned, but it is important to remember that Gabriella is not real," the doctor stresses.

"Try tellin' her that when she in ya face," Penny adds.

"I understand. I really do. But we're finally getting to the root of the problem. Still, Yvonna has been through a lot, and we haven't fully scratched the surface yet. And with this movie coming out about her life, she needs support."

"We're going to be here for her," Jesse adds. "We just need to be sure."

The doctor stands up from her desk and says, "Do you want to see her?"

"I don't want her to know that we're here. I just want to lay my eyes on her, to make sure she's okay," Jesse explains.

"Yeah, I think we wants her to stay focused," Penny offers.

Penny picks up baby Delilah and they all walk down a long, bright hallway to Yvonna's room. They come upon a cream door with a large vertical window. Yvonna is inside reading a book and never looks up to see them there.

"She looks good." Jesse smiles. Ever since she was told her aunt died from cancer, she really wanted to make things work with her sister. She is her only family. "She looks peaceful."

The proud doctor beams. "I knew you'd be pleased."

Baby Delilah coos, and they're worried Yvonna can hear them in the hallway.

"Don't worry, the room is soundproof. We made it that way so that they can have peace against the distractions other patients bring."

Penny looks at Yvonna again and wants to cry. She can also tell by looking at her that she's changed. "It looks like ya program is workin'," Penny says, rocking Delilah lightly.

"It is. Well, let's go over a few more items and I'll let you all go," the doctor says, walking away. Jesse follows and Penny hangs back a little longer to catch another glimpse of Yvonna through the window. But when she does, Yvonna looks at her. Penny smiles at first, but there's something in Yvonna's eyes that's evilly familiar. Penny is frightened.

Not being able to look at Yvonna any longer, she rushes to catch up with the doctor. She holds baby Delilah tightly in her arms. Penny is so panicked that she doesn't see the stolen crystal bird in Delilah's hands.

On the Other Side
of Town

Terrell, Peter, Guy, Jona, and Lily were in a quiet restaurant twenty miles outside of D.C. Their plan to kill Yvonna was foiled after the hit man discovered she was pregnant. The hit man couldn't bring himself to pull the trigger—or, for that matter, give their money back. He said they needed to count it as a loss, considering they didn't provide him with enough information. It didn't matter that they hadn't seen her in months and were surprised that he had even found her so quickly.

Their plan to commit murder and save themselves has changed, but it still would be carried out. The only difference now is that they need to do it themselves.

"So what's this about?" Jona asks Terrell. She's been seeing him lately.

"As you all know, Yvonna committed herself

into a new facility in Virginia. Well, I managed to get ahold of something you all might be interested in."

He picks up a large cylindrical poster holder and removes a sketch, but he does not show the drawing just yet.

"Part of the program for DID is to have the patients describe who they physically see in their minds. I thought this method was particularly groundbreaking, especially for Yvonna, since she'd taken on her father's personality. So how do we know every personality she sees isn't coming from a real person?"

"We don't," Jona replies.

Everyone is interested, because they know it's going somewhere big.

"Well?" Lily says, eyeing the rolled-up sketch. She has gained twenty pounds, and everyone is amazed at how beautiful she is. She has grown her hair out and resembles Eva Mendes a lot. "Show us!"

"One second," he says with his hand out. "Well . . . when they finished with Yvonna, and she gave the artist the details necessary to create a composite drawing of Gabriella, this is what they came up with." He unrolls the sketch and lays it down flat on the table. They all look at it and then back at one another.

"It can't be," Guy says, looking at the sketch and than back at Terrell.

"So you remember this case?" Terrell inquires.

"Remember it? It was all over the fucking news!"

"I don't remember this," Jona says.

"If you gonna hang out with cops, you got to know the cases," Lily states. "This little girl wandered into a Baptist church in D.C. on a Sunday morning about twentysomethin' years ago. The congregation referred to her as an 'angel' because she seemed to have come from the sky. She was there every Sunday for six months faithfully and would always be hungry and dirty."

"Where were her parents?" Jona queries.

"Whenever they would ask her," Guy replies, picking up the tale, "she'd tell them she'd get in trouble if she told them their names. So they kept her secret—fed and took care of her—until one Sunday she didn't show up."

Jona's eyes sadden. "So what did they do?"

"They were devastated," Lily answers. "They had gotten so used to taking care of her that they'd built a room in the basement of their church for her, and everything. She was the church's daughter. They'd bought clothes for her and would send her off with packaged snacks. They said she always took two of everything when she left. It was like she was looking out for somebody else.

"Anyway, they reported her missing, and the media went mad. They hired a forensic artist and, with Pastor Robinson's help, they drew the little girl's picture." She points at the drawing on the table. "It looked awfully like this, and it was put up everywhere. They raised a million-dollar reward to find her."

"Oh, my God," Jona says. "What happened?"

"Nothing," Terrell answers. "They never found her, and the church was never the same."

Jona looks at the picture, trying to remember something. "What was her name?"

Chill bumps run through their spines when they realize that even the name is the same. "G-Gabriella," Terrell manages to say. "They called her Gabriella."

Silence.

"But she looks older in this picture," Peter says. "The same eyes, and even the same face, but just older. How is this possible?"

"Maybe she knew her. All I know is we have to find out," Terrell concludes.

A Maryland home development

"Did you feed Spike?" Lavera Aniston, a twenty-six-year-old African-American woman, asks her son as she turns over steaks on the grill in their backyard. She knows if they don't feed their dog, he'll want theirs.

"No, Mommy," Quentin says, playing with his portable game. "He's already eating."

Lavera walks to the doghouse and screams when she sees him chewing a white female's hand.

Don't miss Mikal Malone's

Pit Bulls in a Skirt

On sale now from Dafina Books

Chapter 1

The Hustlers' Ball

December, Friday, 10:30 P.M.

Mercedes

It had been an hour since I hung up with my mother, and I was still pissed.

I couldn't believe she waited until the last minute to tell me she couldn't watch her own grandkids! Tonight was the wrong night for her to pull this bullshit on me. Mr. Melvin's yearly Christmas party, which we call "the Hustlers' Ball," was in an hour, and it was obvious I wasn't gonna make it.

Mr. Melvin, the property manager, started the parties at the community center in Emerald City to try to stop the violence. However, what he didn't realize was all he did was breed every hustler in D.C. that was in the game. It was the only time we allowed the security guards to open the gates for outsiders, but not without checking the list we provided for them first. We owned Emerald City and everybody in it. Nobody made a move without clearing it with us first. Even though D.C. government paid the guards, they received their *real* orders and *real* money from us.

With five buildings and twelve floors in every one of them, Emerald City was one of the largest projects in the city. Originally named the Frederick Douglass Housing Projects, the project acquired the nickname of Emerald City because all of the buildings had emerald green awnings.

Tucked behind the gates of Emerald City were Murry's food store, a barbershop, a beauty salon, and an arcade—everything you needed, including every kind of drug you could imagine.

"Ma, are you sure you can't watch them for me?" By now, I was begging my mother—something I normally don't do. But for the Hustlers' Ball, it was warranted.

"I'm positive. Bye, Mercedes!"

Click.

She hung up on me! I cannot believe she hung up on me! Man! I can't stand her sometimes!

I opened my bedroom door and walked into the living room. I started contemplating whether I should ask my son, who was sitting on the couch playing a video game, to watch his sisters for me. Asking Cameron Jr. was almost as bad as asking my mother. He had his own mind now, and that was somewhat scary. He was growing up very fast. I knew it was just a matter of time before he wanted in the game and in the life he'd been raised around.

Big Cameron already had him counting the cash we collected at the end of the week from the runners. And as long as he learned the ropes from his father, I had no problem with him dealing when he was ready, but he had to be *ready*. I loved this life and everything about it. Considering the power, the money, and the look on my man's face when he came through the gates and saw shit was still intact, this life excited me. There is no other feeling that can compare—outside of the way Cameron makes me feel when we make love.

"Li'l C, you sure you don't wanna make two hundred dollars tonight?" I asked him while he was playing *Madden* on our fifty-inch plasma-screen TV. "It'll help your momma out a lot."

I sat down and put my arm around him. He looked irritated, and I could tell he knew I was trying to butter him up.

"Doin' what, Ma?" he asked, never taking his eyes off the game.

"Watchin' your sisters," I responded, playing with his hair.

He looked at me with his big eyes and that beautiful curly hair like I had just asked him to do the worst thing in the world. Letting me know he wasn't going for it.

Cameron Jr. was thirteen years old and helped

me out a lot with eight-year-old Chante and four-year-old Baby Crystal, but lately Chante was becoming too much for anyone to handle. And I made a promise not to force him to watch his sisters unless I was handling business, and I always kept my promises.

"Come on, Ma! All Chante gonna do is get on my nerves when you leave! She makes me sick sometimes! She cries the moment you go, plus she don't listen."

"Calm down, boy. I ain't gonna *make* you do anything. But you know the ball's tonight, and your Aunt Stacia and Dex gonna be here in a minute to pick me up."

Truthfully, I could've paid anybody to watch them, but I like them to be around their own things and in their own place. Plus I didn't trust just *anybody* in my apartment. And most of the muthafuckas I knew, who would have jumped at the opportunity to earn two hundred dollars for four hours, were fucking with that shit. So sending my kids with them or letting them watch them at my place was out of the question.

Between all of our clothes and our expensive furniture from overseas, I had over $200,000 worth of shit in my apartment. We did real well with the money the drug life gave us, so I didn't need anybody taking it from me because I messed around and let someone in my apartment who could later plot to rob us.

"If I say 'no,' you gonna be mad?" he asked.

"How can I be mad at you?" I rebutted. As I looked into my son's eyes, it never ceased to amaze me how much he looked like his father. "I'm just gonna be upset, that's all." I continued hoping he'd change his mind.

"Well, I don't wanna do it," he said, continuing to play his game and avoiding my stare.

"All right, then," I said, walking slowly to my room. My tired attempt to give him time to change his mind. "Let me go tell your aunt the bad news."

I walked to my closet, which held Cameron's and my clothes. It was so packed that I could hardly find anything when I wanted it. Looking at the packed closet, I let out a frustrated sigh. I would be so happy when Cameron became a lieutenant, so we could finally move out of Emerald City. The bottom line was this: No matter how much money we had, we were still living in the projects. I knew it, even if the people around me chose to forget.

I grabbed my white Eddie Bauer ski jacket and zipped it up all the way to the top. I was just about to leave my room, until I remembered to grab my Marc Jacobs bag with "My Bitch" tucked inside it. My Bitch was the nickname I gave to the nine millimeter. I never left my house without it. I hadn't had to use her yet, but I was willing to . . . if need be.

I walked toward the elevators. As always, the stench that met my nose reminded me of how nasty my neighbors were. I could immediately smell the dirty apartments and the trash, which sat behind their doors for far too long.

While waiting on the elevator, Derrick, one of the grimiest niggas on my squad, walked up to me. Derrick was a hard worker, but he had a tendency to try me from time to time. I was constantly putting him in his place. At first, I used to tell Big Cameron when Derrick got me wrong, but Cam started getting mad. He said that they'd never respect me if I kept running to him over everything they did. So I started handling stuff on my own, and I only came to him about the big shit.

"What up, Mercedes?" he asked as we both waited on the elevator.

"Nothin'." I did my best to keep my tone even, reminding him that we weren't friends.

"You goin' to the ball tonight?" he asked, still trying to spark up convo.

We stepped into the elevator and I met his stare with one of my own.

"Look." I paused. "You know I'm not with the small talk and shit. So unless we talkin' 'bout business, we ain't talkin'."

"Yeah . . . uh . . . I know," he said as we walked off the elevator. He looked all salty and shit. "I'm just tryin' to be cool with the female I report to, that's all."

I didn't respond. I let him walk ahead of me because I hated people walking behind me, especially somebody as grimy as Derrick. When we approached the exit to the building, I saw my girls on the steps.

Shit! They gonna be blown like shit wit' me.

Before he walked outside, I remembered I didn't find out the status of the dope fiend who gave him fifty dollars in counterfeit cash in exchange for some of the purest heroin in Southeast.

"Derrick!" I yelled before he pushed open the building's door. The cold air hit my face quickly before the door slammed shut again.

He turned around and walked over to me. "Yeah."

"What happened with that head? You handle it?"

"Yeah." He smiled as he smoothed the side of his face with his right hand and grabbed his chin. "We handled that shit. I think his funeral was last week."

"A'ight, but next time, get back with me."

"Yeah . . . okay." He stopped, clearly still upset that he had to take orders from me instead of Cameron, even though it had been over three years now. "I'll try to remember that."

"You *will* remember."

He nodded his head and turned toward the door. When he walked through it, the night air hit me hard. It wasn't a match for my Eddie Bauer jacket, but it was hell on my jean-clad legs. You'd think by now I'd be used to the cold air, since I had to man my post for twelve hours a day for the past three years.

The first thing I saw when I opened the door

were tight-ass cars driving through the gates. *Damn! Rashawn from New York really did get the Lamborghini! She's a lucky muthafucka!*

There were all types of high-end cars navigating the streets. Mercedes-Benzes, which happen to be my favorite, BMWs, Range Rovers, Bentleys, and Acuras flooded Emerald City's gates, heading to the ball. Some playas had gone all out, showing up in chauffeured Navigator and Hummer limousines. Seeing the cars got me horny, and now I was even madder at my mother. For a second I even contemplated *making* Li'l C watch his sisters. But like I said, I never break my promise.

I saw my girls handling business as usual, in designer dresses and fur coats, while waiting for Stacia and Dex to scoop us up. The community center was a ten-minute walk because EC was so big, so we were better off driving, which only took about two minutes.

I laughed when I saw them dressed up while handing out orders in front of the building. And as always, Yvette was the loudest.

"*Look* . . . don't tell me you got it if you don't, Dramon! If shit ain't right when we get back, you might as well leave town. I'm not fuckin' around wit' you!"

"I got it, Yvette," he said, with his hands in his pockets, shaking his head with confidence. "Y'all ain't got shit to be worried about tonight. Me and my soldiers holdin' shit down."

Most of our soldiers were between the ages of

sixteen and twenty-one. Cameron said Dex liked them that way because they showed respect; and above all else, they were hungry for that money. He said the older they got, the more rebellious they became and wouldn't take kindly to women giving them orders. Once they reached that rebellious age, he'd cut 'em off. However, if they were good, he'd put them to work outside Emerald City. He wanted as little distractions for us as possible. I respected his plan, but Yvette didn't give a fuck. She was ready to handle them no matter how damn old they were. And most of the soldiers, if not all, *feared* or *respected* Yvette. She could handle shit with the best of the men.

While Yvette was briefing the soldiers, the others turned around and saw me standing there not dressed for the occasion or the night.

"What you doin'? Why ain't you dressed?" Kenyetta asked as she looked me up and down.

I had to give it to my girl. She was killing a red dress, Fendi heels, and the red-and-black lace mink Fendi purse to match it. Kenyetta was five-seven, with dark, pretty skin and Indian hair, which fell to the middle of her back. Tonight she had it up in a classy bun. Men killed for Kenyetta, but she belonged to Dyson, one of the members of the Emerald City Squad.

"Yeah . . . what's up wit' that, Cedes?" Yvette asked after finishing with the workers, who were now at the bottom of the steps manning the gates. "Go put your shit on. Dex and Stacia will be here in a minute," she continued as she pulled out her compact to check her lipstick.

Yvette wasn't the prettiest—but with the money she earned, and the power she had, she quickly became one of the most wanted women in the projects, along with the rest of us. She was a shortie with big titties and a phat-ass to go with it. We joked all of the time about her being one sandwich away from being overweight. She hadn't always been that way. I guess running Emerald City's gates and leading the soldiers took its toll on her body. She had a smooth amber complexion, and sported a short, spiky haircut. Her hair was always fierce, regardless of what she had going on.

At five feet five inches, she was the meanest bitch you could ever come across. I gave the soldiers leeway on *certain* shit, but Yvette didn't give them any on anything. She was in charge of security and made it clear that she wasn't the one to be fucked with, skirt or not. She would carry any nigga anywhere if the money was fucked up or if they were caught slippin'. Being the baddest bitch, it was only fitting that she fucked with the meanest nigga of the Emerald City Squad. And Thick was the only man who could handle her.

When he came into the room, you couldn't help but respect him. Even the scar on his face made you wonder about the life he led.

"Don't start with me. I'm mad enough as it is," I

said, brushing off their comments. I wasn't in the mood to go into what happened with my two-faced mother.

"Don't start with you? Bitch, tonight is *our* night! This is the only night we get recognized for the shit we go through in EC! Ain't no otha project, outside of Emerald, being held down by bitches!" Carissa insisted.

Carissa was usually laid-back, but not when she felt passionate about something. She looked just like a young Salli Richardson, only better. Her skin was the color of copper, and she didn't have a flaw on her body. Not even a mole. She wore her hair in a jazzy bob, which brushed her cheeks every time she moved. She was beautiful.

The niggas gave her the most shit because she was short and cute; and when they saw her, all they thought about was fuckin'. But just like we all dealt with members of the Emerald City Squad, Carissa was no exception. She was messing with Lavelle. And the niggas around here knew if anybody loved their woman, he did. He wouldn't have a problem putting two to the heads of any niggas who disrespected him or her.

"Go and get dressed!" Yvette insisted. "Stacia just called and said she'll be out front in a minute. They comin' through the gate now."

"I can't roll, y'all. I'm serious," I said, tucking my hands back inside my warm pockets. "My mother can't watch the kids tonight."

"Please say you playin'!" Yvette yelled. "Damn! Call her! I'll see if she'll do it for me."

"Don't waste your time. I tried offering her four large and she still said no."

"So you ain't playin'?" Yvette asked in disbelief.

"Naw, I'm not playin', but I wish I was. She messing with Mr. Brown again and she think I don't know that shit. You know his wife's out of town this week at that Mary Kay convention."

"Mom's wrong as shit," Kenyetta said, shaking her head.

"Tell me about it. But y'all go ahead. Just tell me how it was," I said, trying to hide the fact that I really didn't want them to go without me. We did everything together. And I wanted to see if they would ride or die with me for real.

"Look . . . why don't you let Tina watch 'em?" Yvette suggested.

She already knew the answer to that, so I don't even know why she let it fall out of her mouth.

Tina and her badass kids lived with Yvette from time to time when her mother, who lived across the hallway, put her out. Regardless, there was no way in hell I was letting her watch my kids. Besides, Yvette's apartment was nasty and too junky for my taste. The last time I let Crystal stay over Yvette's, she came back with bumps all over her arms and face. I think they were roach bites, and I was mad as shit with Yvette. I got over it after a while, but I made a promise that it would never happen again.

Yvette's my girl, but she could take better care of her crib. I'm surprised Thick's big ass ain't put her in her place yet.

"Naw, I can't do that. You know I like Li'l C to be at his own house, around his own things."

"You spoil those kids rotten!" Kenyetta said. "And Li'l C damn near runnin' the place." She giggled.

Before we could get into anything else, Stacia and Dex pulled up in front of the building in his silver Hummer. Stacia looked beautiful. Her white fur coat was the first thing I saw before her glossy lips started moving.

"Party night!" she screamed through the open window.

"No, she didn't get the white mink I wanted!" Carissa said. "Dex stay lacing her up!"

"I know. Don't she look beautiful?" I added, trying to hide the fact that I was slightly jealous.

The cold air blowing through the window pushed her long hair into her face and teased her fur coat. Her honey brown skin was flawless. She was so beautiful that no one questioned why Dex chose her. We walked down the steps and by the soldiers who were already guarding Emerald City.

"Hey, baby!" I said as Stacia jumped out and gave us all hugs.

"Hey, you!" Stacia yelled back.

Dex came around to the passenger side to open the doors for us and we hugged him too. Stacia

and Dex was livin' it up for real. They were the Be-
yoncé and Jay-Z of Emerald City and we adored
them. Their relationship was the example we used
when we talked to our men. They all made
promises to move us out of Emerald City, once we
got things tight, but Dex had kept his promise to
Stacia.

Stacia and Dex used to live here in Emerald
City until he became the chief in command and
started pulling in six figures a month. Although
Dex got put on and eventually moved, he didn't
stop showin' love to the rest of us.

He was here so much that we started forgetting
he even moved with Stacia to their eight-bedroom
castle-style home in Alexandria, Virginia.

Dex showed his loyalty, but Stacia was another
story. She used to come by all of the time to sit
with us on the steps of Unit C, like we did before
they moved from the projects. We could talk to
her about anything—from our relationships to
our dreams. And if Stacia could make it happen or
help us, she would. She always had the answers.
When she left, it kinda hurt. Our group had been
dismantled, and it hurt even more when she
stopped coming around as much. Dex started getting kidnap threats about Stacia, and he told her
to cut the visits short. Sometimes she didn't listen.

Instead, she'd just dress down so people

wouldn't recognize her if they saw her sitting with us. But the moment anybody saw the fifth girl posted up in front of Unit C, they'd know exactly who she was, no matter how she tried to disguise herself. We all missed Stacia but understood that Dex kept his promise. We wanted her to be happy.

Dex didn't always have it that way. At one point he ran hand in hand with my boyfriend, Cameron, Dyson, Thick, and Lavelle. But after Dreyfus, our supplier, came in blasting on Tyland Towers, a project a few blocks over from ours, Dex came up with a plan that sealed his position as the man of Emerald City.

They say Dreyfus is six-three, dark-skinned, with smooth black hair. But no matter his looks, he was ruthless. He didn't get involved with every little detail that happened in the projects and hated being bothered with bullshit. The only thing he demanded was his money be right and on time, *every time*. About three years ago, the crew over at Tyland Towers failed to heed his warning.

When some stickup kids from uptown D.C. got the inside scoop from somebody on the inside as to where the warehouse was in Tyland Towers, they took full advantage. They got into the crew for over $200,000 in cash and product that night. And all of that shit was on consignment. When Dreyfus found out that Jamal, who ran Tyland Towers, let some niggas get into him for that much cash, he came through with ten niggas blastin' on Thanksgiving Day.

He killed off all of Jamal's troops and sliced his throat in front of his pregnant girlfriend, Patricia. Then he called a meeting with the captains from all of the spots he supplied. Dex went to represent Emerald City because there was no lieutenant at that time. While they were there, Dreyfus reminded them of his policies, particularly not having his money fucked with, using Tyland Towers as an example. He vowed that shit would be worse if it happened again.

After the meeting Dex came up with the idea of the gatekeepers. He called Cameron, Dyson, Thick, and Lavelle, also known as the Emerald City Squad, and told them about his plan. Instead of them hating, they put the plan into action to ensure what happened to Tyland Towers didn't happen to Emerald City.

The plan consisted of four gatekeepers running the largest unit, Unit C, at all times. Since all of Emerald City could clearly be seen from Unit C, one responsibility of a gatekeeper was to handle "the approach."

The approach happened the moment the security gave the wave that something wasn't right with whoever was coming through. Two people handled that function. The other person handled security and the fourth handled the collection of the funds.

Dex's plan worked so well, that Dreyfus made him the chief of Emerald City. But when the money really started flowing, it became difficult for the EC Squad to man the gates alone. More fiends were coming through, which meant more product and more responsibility. They hadn't anticipated what would happen if things worked out so well. Because of that, they never trained anyone else on the gatekeeper plan, since they didn't trust anyone.

That's when Thick came up with the plan to put us out there. Since we were around them all of the time, they trusted us and we knew Emerald City inside out. That was three years ago, and we've been manning the gate ever since.

"Wow, girl, you wearing jeans?" Stacia asked, tugging at the loop on my belt. "That's different."

"I'm not wearing jeans. . . . I can't go," I said, avoiding the disappointment on my friend's face.

"What? Why?" she asked, looking at Dex, who looked more and more like money every time I saw him. The diamond earring in his right ear was so bright that it almost looked like a flashlight.

"Damn, girl! Does your man know that? I just saw him and he ain't say shit about that," Dex asked with his raspy voice.

"Not yet. I can't find him anywhere. You know how y'all take all day to get ready for the ball. He put more time into tonight than he did on me." I laughed. "Well, look, go ahead and have fun!" I didn't want to continue to throw a pity party outside of Unit C and bring everyone down. "I'll be a'ight."

"We can't leave you," Yvette said. "You know that shit. How we gonna go to the Hustlers' Ball with one of the gatekeepers missin'?"

"But y'all look so nice. Seriously, y'all can go without me." I really wanted them to stay and chill with me, but I knew how bad they wanted to show off their outfits.

"Naw . . . we chillin' wit' you tonight!" Kenyetta said as she hit my arm. "But damn, girl, I was gonna kill them in this dress tonight!" She pouted. "Dyson woulda been mad at my ass when I came through them doors. He needs to be thankin' you," she continued as she opened her fur coat revealing her red dress. I could tell that if you shined the right light on it, you would've been able to see right through it.

"You? I wanted to show mine off too!" Carissa opened her coat, revealing her short black Missoni dress under her fur coat, which cost over two grand. "They wasn't gonna be ready for what I was gonna give."

"Well, since we're having a fashion show," Yvette said, "I was gonna kill 'em in my dress too." Yvette's white-on-white look made her look sexy and sophisticated. The full-length fur coat set off

326

her Emilio Pucci dress gracefully. They all looked like a million bucks. And for what? To stay home. "Anyway . . . go ahead, Stacia. We'll see you later."

"Well, okay, guys!" Stacia sighed. "I hope y'all know you're breakin' my heart. How you gonna leave me with the guys alone?"

"You can handle 'em." Carissa laughed. "And keep a close eye on my man."

"I'll try." She laughed back. "I'm gonna call y'all tomorrow!" Stacia said as Dex hugged us, then opened the door for her. "Don't forget about the cookout and bring my babies! *All* of them, Mercedes!"

"Okay . . . I will." I waved.

"I have a surprise for them too," she continued to say as she jumped into the truck, and Dex got behind the wheel. "I love y'all!"

"We love you too! Have fun!" We waved as they drove to the party.

"Sorry, y'all. I know how bad you guys wanted to go," I said, happy they decided to stay. I figured the least I could do was get them high. "Well, since we got the soldiers at the gates tonight, let's crack open the Ace of Spades I have in my apartment on chill. Plus Big Cameron left me a phat-ass J too," I said as we walked up the steps.

"I'm wit' that shit!" Carissa said, smiling.

"Me too," Yvette added, linking her arm with Kenyetta's. "As long as we got each other, I'm good."

Even though we didn't make it to the ball, we still had a nice time laughing and talking about old times.

We were still up at four in the morning when the phone rang. No one expected to hear what we did when I answered the phone.

And the news would change our lives forever.